EYE CANDY

Dorie Graham

TORONTO • NEW YORK • LONDON
AMSTERDAM • PARIS • SYDNEY • HAMBURG
STOCKHOLM • ATHENS • TOKYO • MILAN • MADRID
PRAGUE • WARSAW • BUDAPEST • AUCKLAND

This dedication goes to Theresa and Ray Buckley for their steadfast love and support through all the ups and downs of my life. Wherever you each may travel, in whatever realm you may walk, a part of my heart goes with you. I love you always.

ISBN 0-373-79134-8

EYE CANDY

This edition published by arrangement with Harlequin Books S.A.

www.eHarlequin.com

Printed in U.S.A.

"Ready to try on something else?"

Sam's voice melted over Crystal like warm honey. There was something different in his tone, something...enticing.

She blinked, banishing the thought. Her imagination was running wild, trying to make him into a mystery man. This was *Sam*. He hadn't gone through any transformation. He was still her friend, as reliable and trustworthy as ever.

"Sure. Can I model what I put on? I know nothing about lingerie and I need a guy's perspective."

His jaw set and he pushed away from the dressing room door. "You don't have to model for me. And you don't need my opinion. You decide what you like."

Frustration welled up inside her. "But I need to know what *you* think is sexy. Can't you just come in here and tell me honestly how I look?"

"Crystal, I'm a man and you're a hot woman asking me to watch you in your dressing room where you'll be slipping into lingerie designed to entice. You have to know that just the thought of it has me so turned on, I can hardly see straight."

Heat rushed to her cheeks. He was turned on. By her. A shiver of excitement ran through her. "If that's the case, Sam, I think you better get in here."

Dear Reader,

I'm so pleased to share my next Blaze novel with you. Thanks to the support of our loyal readers, the Harlequin Blaze line is going strong. I'm ecstatic to be a part of it.

I had been toying with the idea of writing about a hero who was hopelessly in love with a heroine, who was hopelessly in love with another man, or at least thought she was. I added a Blaze story twist inspired by the submissive lyrics of "Barbie Girl," by Aqua and this story was born.

When tomboy Crystal Peterson asks good friend and men's magazine publisher Sam Schaffer to make her over to audition for a lingerie calendar her motive is to catch the eye of the photographer involved. As Sam transforms Crystal, though, their relationship heats up and soon she is wondering whose eye candy she wants to be.

I hope you enjoy this story as much as I have. As always, it's been a pleasure. Look for my SEXUAL HEALING miniseries in 2005. Meanwhile, I'd love to hear from you. You can write me at P.O. Box 769012, Roswell, GA 30076, or e-mail me at dorenegraham@mindspring.com.

Happy Reading,

Dorie Graham

Books by Dorie Graham

HARLEQUIN BLAZE

39—THE LAST VIRGIN
58—TEMPTING ADAM

1

HE LOOKED GOOD ENOUGH to eat. Crystal Peterson drew in a breath of the early-spring air as desire bloomed in her. Sunlight dappled Ron Kincaid's golden hair and played off the contours of his biceps and thighs. He advanced with the other players up the field in Atlanta, Georgia's Piedmont Park, each ripple of muscle sending warmth twisting through her. The man might be a photographer during the week, but on the weekends he had all the right moves.

A shout drew Crystal's gaze from the object of her affections, calling her attention back to her own teammates. Sam Schaffer, her longtime friend and confidante, launched the football in a neat spiral. It sailed toward her. She leaped, hands outstretched.

This was her chance.

If she played this right, she'd have everyone's attention—including Ron's. Rough leather stung her palms and a feeling of excitement gripped her. As many times as she and Sam had been through this drill, it never ceased to amaze her when she caught the damn ball.

She ran.

Ron pounded down the turf after her. Keenly aware that all eyes were on her, especially Ron's, she kicked forward with everything she had. The makeshift end zone, marked by two park benches, yawned ahead of her, the way amazingly clear. Her heart quickened. She could make this touchdown. She could win the game.

Surely Ron would notice her then.

Someone went down with a loud thump behind her to her left, but she could still feel Ron in hot pursuit. He was close, too close.

He's going to catch me.

A thrill raced through her. *His heat pressed in behind her as her heart tripped wildly. In one swift motion, he took her down, rolling to soften the fall, cradling her in his arms. The solid planes of his body pressed into her, his chest firm against her back, his breath hot in her ear and the hard ridge behind his fly nestled in the cleft of her bottom. She turned her head, so his mouth brushed across her cheek, then whispered along her lips—*

"Go right!" Sam yelled from somewhere in the distance behind Ron, yanking her from her reverie.

She swerved to the right. As always, Sam was covering her back. She had been following his lead ever since that day in the first grade, when he had helped her outmaneuver a bully on the playground. Three years of their old high-school gang meeting in the park for these Saturday games had only ingrained the instinct.

If anyone could take out Ron, it was Sam.

The end zone loomed just out of reach. Her lungs burned and her legs ached. Shouts rose all around her. She could feel Ron hot on her tail. Close. She imagined him reaching out, his fingertips brushing the rolled waistband of her sweats. The temptation to let him catch her swept over her, but she shrugged it off.

With a primal yell, she dived for the end field. She hit the earth hard, clutching the football to her chest and rolling. Shouts and hoots of victory rose up around her. She fell to her back, gulping in huge drafts of air.

She'd made it. They'd won the game.

Ron moved into the patch of blue above her, breathing hard himself, his cheeks ruddy and his hair appealingly windblown. "You're fast, Peterson."

Euphoria rose in her and exploded in a wide grin. He knew her name.

Before she could manage a reply, he sauntered away, spreading his smile and his charm to the number of female admirers who'd watched him from the sidelines. They surrounded him now, evidently oblivious to Crystal's double victory.

She rose up on her elbows and cocked her head, squinting against the sun to be sure he showered his attention equally on each of his companions, without focusing on any one of them. All appearances indicated he was still single and unattached. Though it rankled to see so many women pawing him, she couldn't quite blame them.

The man had charisma.

Her teammates and friends closed in on her. A gorgeous brunette, one of the newcomers to the group, hovered near Sam. Not surprising, since she bore the long legs and sultry appearance that distinguished all of Sam's women.

Only she wasn't technically one of Sam's women. She had thrown out the bait, all right, but Sam wasn't biting, which came as a surprise. He'd never been one for serious relationships, though it seemed lately he wasn't even going for the casual ones.

Crystal shook her head. She had been watching poor damsels fall by the wayside ever since Sam hit his stride sometime in the seventh grade. Thank God she'd built up a natural immunity by then.

She tilted her head as he approached. The wind had ruffled his sand-colored hair, his green eyes shone and, though he rarely smiled, he somehow greeted everyone with warmth. He would make some girl a good catch. If not for his stubborn streak and cynical outlook, she herself might have been interested.

He offered her his hand, his eyes tinged with a curious note of censure. What was bothering him? Hadn't she just helped them win their first victory in weeks? Ignoring the look, she let him pull her to her feet.

"Good catch," he said.

"Good pass."

Her eyes wide, the brunette by his side plucked a tuft of grass from Crystal's hair. "You were marvelous. My heart was in my throat. I didn't think you'd make it, until you dove at the last minute. I could never dive into the ground like that."

"Thanks." Crystal smiled a tight smile.

No, this woman wasn't the type to risk breaking one of her well-manicured nails. She seemed a bit on the fragile side, ethereal in her beauty. Crystal squelched the smidgen of envy that crept over her. What did she need with delicate beauty, when she'd just scored the winning touchdown?

Grinning, she turned toward the crowd of familiar

faces. Mike Steels, their linebacker, and his wife, Paige, who'd warred through high school, then surprised them all by getting married right after college, beamed at her, their two-year-old daughter bouncing on Steels's hip.

"Hey, Crystal, that was awesome!" Steels, his blond hair cropped close to his scalp, high-fived her with his free hand. "We're naming number two after you."

Paige shook her own blond head as she rubbed the small bulge in her stomach. "I'm not sure *he* would like that, but you were awesome, Crystal, just like always. Where's that sister of yours?"

Frowning, Crystal scanned the remaining clusters of people. Had she been so wrapped up in Ron, she hadn't noticed Megs had no-showed? "She's probably just busy with that man of hers. They spend all their free time together."

"Tell her we missed her," Paige said.

"Hey, quit hogging the star player." Another of the guys in their group, who'd taken Crystal on her first car date in the tenth grade, picked her up, then swung her in a wide circle. "That's the way to do it, Peterson. I taught you well."

She laughed and threw Sam a glance. Had he just been glaring at the back of their friend's head? He wore his usual guarded expression, but for a split second she'd thought she'd glimpsed a flash of anger. Though he had spent endless hours practicing one-on-one with her, readying her for these games, he wasn't usually so touchy. He was a master at masking his emotions. Only after years of deciphering his subtle body language could she tell when something was bothering him.

She sighed. His shoulders were tense and his jaw set. Something must really be upsetting him. She'd have to soothe his ruffled feathers later.

"We're the best!" Her friend whooped and set her down.

The rest joined in his enthusiasm, each adding his or her own victory yell. Crystal grinned, letting her gaze scan the crowd. They'd all been through a lot, the gang. Some had moved on to different graduate schools, a couple had taken off to Europe, but somehow, they had managed to keep in touch. It was great having so many of them still together after all these years.

When the noise died down and everyone started drifting apart, she finally turned to Sam, no longer able to hold in her happy news. "Ron said I was fast. He said my name. He knows who I am."

Sam frowned. "Of course he knows your name. You and Cami are the only two women who ever play. Believe me, *all* the guys are very aware of who you are."

It was true. Megs and the rest of the girls who'd cheered their high-school football team through the state championship carried on their tradition of livening up the sidelines. Crystal had never been one to sit idly during a game, though. She had to be part of the action. So did Cami. Maybe that was why they'd been friends since junior high. That, and Cami appreciated her newfound admiration of Ron.

"Well, don't be such a spoilsport," Crystal said to

Sam. "As my friend, you're supposed to be happy for me."

"As your friend, I'll tell you one more time he isn't your type."

"And what does that mean? How do you know what my type is?"

"Please, who's listened to you moan and groan about every guy you've ever had a crush on, since junior high?"

"Fine, but maybe I'm ready to change my type. I won't know, though, until I get to know him, which you could help with. You two go way back. In fact, I'm still not clear how you knew him in high school and I didn't. How come you never hooked us up?"

He shrugged. "We had some classes together. And I never hooked you up then, for the same reason I won't help you now. I know him, and I just don't see the two of you hitting it off. It's a waste of time."

"You're so sweet." She patted his cheek. "But I refuse to take such a pessimistic view. This is progress."

Camille Everett slung her arm around Crystal's shoulders, her blue eyes sparkling, her short, bottle-black hair spiking out in fashionably odd angles. Cami had worn "bed head" long before it'd become popular. "That's my girl. Taught her everything she knows," she said to Sam, winking.

"Right, Cami," Crystal teased. "That's why I fumble so well."

"Smart-ass."

"At least I have an ass."

"Well, it doesn't have to be a bubble butt to qualify. Parker likes my ass just fine."

"Sam," Crystal demanded, "Do you think I have a bubble butt?"

"Let's see." He turned her. "It's hard to tell in those sweats and without a more in-depth assessment…"

She glared at him. Of course, he'd teased her like this hundreds of times in his dry, humorless way. He didn't mean anything by it, but the lanky brunette's hurt look drew a spurt of empathy. Poor thing. Sam would have to find a way to let her down easy.

He shrugged as if to say, "Can't blame a guy for trying," then said, "It's nicely rounded, but *bubble butt* doesn't do it justice. How about *bountiful butt?*"

She shoved him.

A lock of his sand-colored hair fell over his eye. He swept it aside and came as close to grinning as he ever came—a slight tightening of his lips. "It was a compliment. I think you have a great ass."

"Thank you. And I like my sweats. How the hell would I play in anything else? A girl's got to be able to move."

His gaze swept over her rumpled T-shirt and sweats and her tousled ponytail. "I've always liked the way you dress. You don't worry about what anyone thinks. It shows a certain confidence."

"That from the publisher of *Edge,* the trendiest men's magazine in the Southeast. You should be flattered," Cami said to Crystal.

"You're right. The magazine is doing well, isn't it? Tell Cami about the award you're up for," Crystal urged Sam.

"The National Magazine Awards. It's great that we're in the running. I don't see us winning this year, but I really think we've got a shot at next year's, if I can find a new columnist. Someone to give a woman's point of view on some of the more weighty issues."

Cami's silver laughter filled the air. "You mean people actually read the articles?"

Stiffening, Sam stared at her. Her eyes rounded. "I would read articles on women's issues...probably."

Crystal groaned. He'd been hedging about this for weeks. If she'd known what he was really after, she would never have done that piece on fantasy dates for him. His readers had eaten it up. She still received fan mail on it. "I'm sure you'll find someone. There are lots of female writers out there who'd give anything for the opportunity."

"You could do it." His voice held such certainty that for a second she almost believed him.

Then she came to her senses. "I'm on a deadline right now, then I have that makeover series *Woman's Day* is interested in. It's a whole new area for me."

"Sooner or later you're going to get tired of writing all that fluff."

"Award-winning fluff," Cami clarified.

"All the more reason to try something with a little bite. Whatever happened to the girl who was going to change the world with the stroke of her pen?" Sam's green gaze pinned Crystal with a challenge.

Everything in her wanted to rise to that challenge. The memory of a long-ago campfire flickered in her mind. The night had been clear, the stars bright. At fifteen, everything had seemed possible. Somehow, sharing her dreams with Sam had made them feel more attainable.

But she'd tried her hand at a few serious articles in the past. They had all been rejected so fast it had made her head spin. She could certainly use the steady income Sam's columnist position would pay, but did she have it in her? Besides, Cami was right. Her fluff pieces did well, well enough to pay the bills.

She finally turned to him. "She grew up and wised up."

"You could start with the lighter content, like that last piece, then work your way into the heavier stuff."

Again, the prospect tempted her, but ultimately he wanted the meatier articles. She'd built a reputation on diet dilemmas and decorating disasters. Would readers, let alone editors, accept anything else from her? Maybe she was meant to fulfill the world's fluff quota.

Rather than argue with him, she opted for a diversionary tactic, one that had always worked well in the past. "Look, I'm parched. Who's going to buy me a beer?"

SUNLIGHT STREAKED in a slant through a side window, casting long shadows across the scarred table. The Red Hot Chili Peppers rocked over the hubbub of the crowded bar. The smell of cigarette smoke and beer invoked memories of countless other Saturday afternoons.

Sam took a long draw from his bottle of Corona. Crystal had looked good out there today. He let his gaze drift over her as she sat beside Cami, opposite him in a booth. Next to him, the brunette whose name he couldn't remember said something about a sale at

Phipps Plaza, but he found himself too distracted to listen.

That old familiar hum started low in his gut at the sight of Crystal's flushed cheeks and bright eyes. Never had he seen eyes so blue. Sometimes, such excitement and clarity filled them, it almost hurt to look at her.

He gripped his beer as she glanced two tables over at Ron Kincaid, her eyes filled with longing. Sam shook his head, biting back a curse. The guy had distracted her today on the field, too. This was one crush that seemed to be more than a passing fancy. Even Kincaid, as jaded as he was, was destined to appreciate the treasure he'd have in Crystal. Was Sam so wrong not to help her connect with the man?

Kincaid was a decent guy, one of the best freelance photographers Sam knew. He had used him a number of times on shoots, but the guy changed women as often as he changed socks. Crystal was so different from other women, Sam couldn't imagine the guy not falling for her unique beauty. Even with a guarantee Kincaid wouldn't hurt her, would Sam hook her up with him? Just the thought of it sent a wave of possessiveness over him.

He tamped down on feelings he'd long ago suppressed. Feelings he'd revealed to Crystal in his misguided youth. It had been the summer he'd turned fifteen. They'd gone camping, the group of them—Cami, Steels, Crystal, Sam and the rest. Crystal had recruited him to go foraging for firewood with her, while the others explored a nearby lake.

He and Crystal had talked while they gathered the dry wood, then built the fire, Crystal going on with her plans for college. She'd had a cousin who'd attended Florida State, so she'd set her sights on enrolling there. By the end of the trip she'd convinced them all, enticing them with the lure of "out-of-state." She'd instigated the exodus to Florida, and Sam, missing the grand variety and international flavor of Atlanta, had led the migration home again after graduation.

That day in the woods with Crystal had started their future together, though it hadn't quite turned out to be the future he envisioned at the time. As she'd shared her dreams about her life in college, then her career as a journalist, her eyes had glowed. Her face had taken on a radiant flush.

She'd never looked more beautiful.

"I'll have a syndicated column where I'll keep the American public informed of all the important issues. I'll get an apartment, one of those sky-rises in Buckhead, where I can see the heart of Atlanta from my twentieth-story window," she'd said.

Crystal had turned to Sam, her hair, still that rare white-blond, held tame in her usual ponytail. "I'm going to make a hell of a journalist. Communication, that's what's really important."

He'd been so moved by her enthusiasm and he'd wanted to communicate—to share the secret that burned in him. The words spilled out, before he'd had a chance to form them in his head. "I'm in love with you."

A bird cawed somewhere above them. The wind, pungent with the scent of pine, caught the treetops, rattling their leaves. Crystal sat silently beside him, her speech halted by his irrational confession.

He hadn't known what to say, his heart bleeding and exposed. He sat staring at the ground, wishing desperately that it would open up and swallow him.

It hadn't.

"But we're just friends...besides we're too young to know what love is," she'd said at last. Then she'd laughed and punched him in the shoulder. "That's funny, Sam. You really had me going."

He'd swallowed past the lump in his throat, past the unbearable ache in his chest. Hadn't he learned not to expose his feelings? Growing up with his single dad hadn't been easy, but the hardest part had been watching his father pursue women, his heart on his sleeve, only to have them cruise quickly out of his life. The man hadn't learned with Sam's mother, but Sam had taken note.

He hadn't ever been that certain someone for Crystal and, in all this time, it didn't appear as if he'd ever be. Still, sometimes he felt he was just biding his time with the different women he'd been involved with, always careful never to make promises he couldn't keep. Generally, that made for short relationships, but he'd never minded any of them walking away.

"Hey, Parker. What were you doing working on a Saturday? Trying to make the rest of us look bad?" Crystal's voice dragged Sam back to the present as Parker Scott, Cami's accountant boyfriend, slid into the booth across from him.

"We're getting into tax season. If I don't get caught up now, I'll be buried in a month's time. Then I won't get to see my squeeze." He scooped Cami to his side and kissed her thoroughly.

Sam shook his head at the blatant display and Crystal sighed.

"Must be nice," the brunette beside him murmured and gave Sam a speculative look.

He set down his beer. He hadn't done anything to lead her on, but somehow she hadn't gotten the hint. Maybe he'd have to be less subtle.

Cami and Parker finally emerged for air. She stabbed her finger at his chest. "You'd better make time for me, tax season or not."

"Of course I will, honey." He glanced around the table, then grinned at her. "I've got a surprise for you."

"You do? What?"

"It's what we were talking about last night."

"What were we talking about last night?"

"You know."

Her eyes rounded. "The makeover?"

"You still want to do it?" He placed an envelope in her hands. "It's a gift certificate for Allure Imaging, where they fix you up, then take your picture. I figure it's a place to start. They do wardrobe, makeup and hair consultations, so you can decide exactly what the new you will be."

"Oh, I've done that." The brunette pressed her hands together. "They did a fabulous job. Just as good as any I've seen in *Cosmo.* You worked for them, didn't you, Sam?"

"I interned in the fashion department."

Crystal turned to Cami, a frown marring her forehead. "What new you?"

"Cami's tired of all the guys thinking of her as…well, as one of the guys."

"No, I'm not. I don't mind them treating me that way. I just don't want *you* to forget that I'm all woman."

Parker put his face so close to hers, their noses rubbed. "There is no way that's going to happen. All your womanly traits are very obvious to me, no matter how you choose to camouflage them." He plucked at her oversize T-shirt.

"What do you mean camouflage?" Crystal glanced down at her own clothes.

Sam shook his head, smiling inwardly at her look of dismay. One of the things he loved about her was that she'd never been self-absorbed.

"No offense, Crystal," Parker said. "You two do dress alike. It doesn't bother me one bit, but she brought it up. I just agreed."

Crystal swung her gaze to Cami, who threw her hands up defensively. "You gave me the idea when you were talking about pitching that series to *Woman's Day.*"

"But I wasn't talking about you."

"Still, you got me thinking. We do kind of dress..."

"We dress like the guys?" Crystal finished for her.

Her stunned look nearly had Sam laughing. How anyone could mistake Crystal for one of the guys was a mystery to him. As far as he was concerned, nothing she could do would detract from her feminine allure.

"You dress for comfort—jeans, sweats, T-shirts."

"Like the guys," Crystal repeated, a look of amazement spreading across her face.

The brunette pressed her lips together.

"So, what's shaking?" Mike Steels pulled a chair

up to the end of the table, then dropped his bulk in it.

''Steels.'' Sam toasted him with his beer. He and Steels went back almost as far as he and Crystal. They'd swept the local T-ball league together way back when. ''The girls are talking makeovers.''

''No, we're not.'' Crystal folded her arms across her chest and slumped in her seat.

''No one said you had to do it, too,'' Cami argued. She grinned at Parker. ''I think it'll be fun. Wait until you see the new sexy me.''

''Hey, Cam.'' Steels leaned forward, his hair spiked to a hard edge. ''You having a sexy makeover?''

She waved the gift certificate. ''Looks that way.''

''Awesome. Maybe you can be one of Kincaid's calendar hotties.''

''What calendar hotties?'' Parker asked.

Steels glanced over his shoulder, toward where Kincaid sat flanked by a blonde and a brunette. ''He's shooting a lingerie calendar. He's looking for twelve hot babes to model sexy lingerie for it.'' He shook his head. ''The guy has got one tough job.''

''No thanks.'' Cami snuggled closer to Parker. ''This makeover is for my honey only.''

''That's right.'' Parker wrapped a protective arm around her. ''She'll be modeling her new lingerie for me and me alone.''

Steels shrugged. ''I don't think he'll have any trouble finding the models he needs. He's always got plenty of them making over him.''

Crystal bristled on the other side of Cami. A small growl of discontent escaped her. Sam followed her glare to where two more beautiful brunettes had planted themselves at Kincaid's table.

"Come on, Crystal, you're a hottie," Sam couldn't help but assure her.

Both Crystal and the brunette beside him turned wide-eyed looks his way. He lifted his hands in appeal. "It isn't the clothes that make a woman. It's the woman who makes the clothes."

"Really?" A note of exasperation punctuated Crystal's voice.

Sam held her gaze. How could she not know she was one of the world's sexiest women? "Yes."

"Great. I must do wonders for my low riders." She popped up in her seat and turned to Cami and Parker. "I'm going shopping. Could you guys let me out?"

"Come on, stick around." Sam reached for her hand.

The brunette nudged him with her elbow. "She wants to shop. Let her go."

He blew out a breath as Crystal freed herself from the booth. *Shopping?* Though it wasn't unlike her to set off at the drop of a hat, she *never* shopped. She must be upset.

She turned and saluted them. "It's been great. Catch you guys later."

"I'll walk you out." Sam started to rise, but the brunette clutched at his arm, her eyes issuing an ultimatum.

"Sam, don't, or..."

"Or what?"

"Or I won't be here when you get back."

He gave her a long, appraising stare. Well, at least

this time *he* was doing the walking away. "I guess I'll have to take my chances."

With a nod to Cami, Parker and Steels, Sam strode after Crystal. He caught up with her in the parking lot. She looked upset and forlorn. Shoving his hands into his pockets to keep from reaching for her, he called to her, "Hey, want some company?"

She stopped with her hand on the car door. Her gaze met his and all the confusion and hurt in her eyes drew him another step closer. She said, "I'm going shopping."

Was she that shook up over Kincaid? Sam stared at her for a long moment, the desire to pull her into his arms and comfort her overwhelming. He'd never been able to deny her wishes, though, and he couldn't now.

"I heard," he finally said. "Call me later if you need me. I'll be around."

"Hey." Her eyes narrowed on him. "You okay?"

"Me?"

She nodded. "You seemed a little…peeved today. Everything all right? Nothing new with your dad?"

"No. He's fine. Everything's fine."

"You're sure?"

"Sweetheart, I am the last person you need to worry about."

"Okay. I'm off then." She gave him a quick hug. She stepped into her car, then drove away.

THE SUN DIPPED LOW on the horizon. A breeze stirred through the open car windows, bringing with it the sweet scent of honeysuckle as Crystal pulled into the mall parking lot. A horn blared in the distance. She frowned and slammed her car into park.

Ron had shown up at their weekly games around six weeks ago. To her surprise, he and Sam had known each other, but with an uncharacteristic belligerence, Sam had refused to help set her up with his old acquaintance.

In spite of her own efforts in all that time, the man had barely spoken to her. Humiliation burned through her. He'd hardly noticed her because he saw her as one of the guys. Why hadn't she ever realized it?

Because she never gave her appearance a second thought. The most she used her mirror for was to make sure her ponytail was straight. Usually, she did that by feel.

She got out of the car, then smoothed down her T-shirt. Her hair was still damp from the quick shower she'd taken after leaving the bar, so she'd left it loose for a change. She just hadn't been able to sit there and watch those women fawn over him.

Now that she understood the problem, the solution was easy. Cami may have been on to something. Maybe this makeover idea wasn't so bad, after all. Crystal could certainly use the experience in her upcoming articles.

All she had to do was help Ron to see that she wasn't one of the guys. And the best way to do that was to show him she was every bit as sexy as any one of his calendar models.

In fact...she slowed as she approached the mall entrance...she could *be* one of his calendar models. The idea hit her with breathtaking force.

She'd make herself over—do up her makeup and

hair, dress in something sexy, then she'd have dinner at the restaurant Jules said Ron frequented. She'd eat there every night if she had to, until she "bumped" into him. Once he noticed her, she'd seg into the subject of the calendar and they'd schedule a trial shoot.

How could she go wrong? There she'd be, the focus of his attention, while he snapped his pictures and encouraged her to pose different ways. The man would be hers.

She could do it. She could be one of Ron's calendar hotties.

2

SHE COULDN'T DO IT. Crystal groaned as she stared at her reflection in horror. What had she been thinking? Her cheeks flamed as she gazed at the red corset. Her breasts heaved over the top, her nipples bared for all to see. Either this gadget was ten sizes too small or she'd managed to find the most risqué outfit in the shop.

Aggravated, she yanked off the garment, then discarded it on the pile occupying the small bench in the dressing room. All this time and not a single item would do. When it came to lingerie, she was obviously handicapped.

None of the sizes seemed to work and when she thought she finally had close to the right size, she couldn't figure out if she had the thing on right side up, upside down or backward. How could this be so difficult? No matter how hard she tried, she couldn't seem to pull together the classy look she'd envisioned modeling for Ron.

And she'd rather die than ask that snooty saleswoman for help again. The woman had acted quite put out when Crystal had asked her to help locate her size in some of the garments, then had disappeared before they had finished. Crystal's meager attempt to regain her assistance had only met with failure. Apparently the woman was busy assisting customers of a higher caliber.

Crystal scowled at the pile of clothes. What was she going to do? It'd been so long since she'd shopped for clothes—and she'd never set foot in a lingerie shop before today—that she'd lost the hang of it. Picking out clothes seemed a task one had to have some practice at. She'd spent hours amassing the pile she'd just tried on.

"Damn, how am I supposed to do this?" Frustration welled up inside her.

Allure Imaging was out of the question. They seemed directed more at surface change. That would never fool Ron. She had to do more than change her appearance. Looking sexy wasn't going to get her a spot in that calendar, not up against professional lingerie models.

If Crystal was going to have any chance, clothes wouldn't be enough. She also had to overhaul her personality. She had to become a sex goddess, one so hot and sultry, Ron wouldn't notice the other models.

But she couldn't pull off such a feat by herself. What she needed was someone with fashion experience, who worked with sexy women on a daily basis, who dated sexy women at every opportunity, who liked sexy women and understood their every nuance. She needed someone who had a proven track record with *Cosmo* and *Edge*, magazines at the heart of an industry that used sex to generate its vast income.

She needed someone she trusted, who had the knack for pulling off this kind of transformation.

She needed Sam.

"YOU DON'T NEED ME." Sam blew out a breath and sank back against the leather sofa that took up almost an entire wall of his den.

Disappointment flickered through him. He had been mildly surprised to answer his door to find Crystal standing on his front step. She didn't visit often. He should have been suspicious.

"But I do. You're the only one who can help. Just think about it." Her eyes held a note of pleading, but he mustered his resolve.

No way was he going to help her fix herself up to be eye candy for Kincaid.

She leaned forward, her breasts pressing against the soft cotton of her T-shirt. Her hair, loose for the first time he could remember, fell long and silky over her shoulders as she clenched her hands together. "I can't do this on my own. I tried. Besides, you worked for *Cosmo.* You helped put together all those fashion shows, with those sexy models. You know women. You date sexy women and you feature them all over your magazine. You're the perfect candidate."

He rose, then started to pace across the soft carpet. "You look great as you are. If Kincaid can't see that, he isn't worth the trouble."

"That's my call."

"It's a bad call."

An unladylike snarl escaped her. "I'm just one of the guys to him."

"And what's wrong with that?"

Her eyebrows arched, as if to say she thought he had lost his mind. "I want him to see that I am a *female.* That I am just as good as any one of those models that he dates—that I'm even better."

"Of course you're better. And you don't need to be in any calendar to prove it." He raised his hands in appeal. "Can't you see that you have a down-to-earth appeal that's ten times sexier than any model's?"

"I see." The muscles in her jaw twitched. She sat with her gaze fixed on the floor.

"Good."

"You don't think I can do it."

The note of defeat in her voice tore at him. "Crystal, I didn't say that," he said quietly.

"You didn't have to." She rose, then stood for a moment, fingering her car keys. "Thanks anyway. I'll figure something out."

He walked her to the door, his stomach twisting. The clean soapy scent of her teased his nostrils, but he took little joy in it. Her disappointment seemed to hover over them like a dark cloud.

Damn Kincaid. In that moment, Sam almost wished the photographer *would* notice Crystal, to prove to her she was desirable just as she was.

The door creaked as Sam yanked it open. "I'll call you later."

"Yeah." She turned toward him, hesitating as though she meant to hug him.

They always hugged. They hugged hello. They hugged goodbye. It had been a part of the rhythm of their lives.

He reached for her, but she'd already turned, heading out the door. He gritted his teeth, his fist clenched against the doorjamb. Regret filled him and a tightness constricted his chest. Slowly, her back ramrod straight, she descended his front steps.

A sense of loss swept over him. Before Ron came along, Sam had never said *no* to her. He hated disappointing her now, but, in this case, he had no choice. Couldn't she see that he couldn't help her make herself over for anyone else—not when he still wanted her for himself?

THE SUN HAD LONG SINCE SET by the time Crystal reached her complex. The loud chirping of cicadas rose and fell as she climbed the stairs to her second-floor apartment. Somewhere in the distance, along the Chattahoochee River, the rhythmic mating calls of frogs joined in the chorus. The dank smell of the river drifted on the wind.

Light blazed from every window of her apartment.

"Megs, what are you doing here?" Crystal asked under her breath as she wrestled the key into the lock.

When she'd moved into this apartment on her own, she'd given her younger sister a spare key, so she could drop in whenever she needed to get away from her roommates. Megs was sweet and gentle and everyone's ideal person, but she tended to thrive on drama. All Crystal wanted right now was to collapse into her favorite chair and veg out in front of the TV. She had her own wounds to lick.

How could Sam have turned her down? He was the perfect solution. Somehow, she had to convince him to help her. Maybe she should have offered to pay him for his time and trouble or struck some kind of trade, like cleaning for him or doing his laundry for a month.

Feeling drained, she pushed open the door. The buttery scent of popcorn permeated the air as she stepped into the small entryway. The bang of cupboards and drawers being opened, then shut sounded from the kitchen. Sure enough, her sister's tennis shoes sat in perfect alignment beside the potted plant by the door.

Sighing, Crystal slipped off her own shoes, kicking them haphazardly beside Megs's, trying not to notice how the tatters and stains on her footwear contrasted with the pristine condition of her sister's.

Competing with Megs's perfection had never been an option. Even at the age of three, when Crystal had first laid eyes on the gentle bundle of her sister, she'd somehow sensed she'd been bested before she began. Megs hadn't disappointed her, growing up to be the favorite daughter, the best student and the most popular girl at school.

Funny how the lack of competition had eliminated most of the sibling rivalry between them. Crystal couldn't help but love and admire her sister, who was a genuinely nice person, in spite of all her perfection.

"Crystal, I can't find the chocolate sauce. Please don't tell me you're out."

Megs leaned against the kitchen doorjamb, her eyes puffy, and her nose red. She'd been crying. Well, she was almost perfect. She did tend to overdramatize every little event in her life. Where this trait proved an irritation in other people, though, in Megs it seemed to draw out one's protective instincts.

"It's in the fridge door, hon." Crystal scooped an arm around her sister and turned her toward the refrigerator. "What's wrong?"

A short sniffle escaped Megs. She found the chocolate sauce, then poured it liberally over a bowl of ice cream. "Want some?"

"No thanks. Is it Leo?"

"They offered him the job." She jammed her spoon into the sweet concoction.

"The one in New York?"

Megs nodded.

"But you knew he'd take it, if they offered it. I thought you agreed it was a great opportunity for him. Aren't they paying him big bucks?"

Megs nodded again and stuffed a spoonful of ice cream in her mouth. She turned abruptly, then walked into the living room, where she plopped down on one of Crystal's huge throw pillows on the floor by the fireplace. A half-eaten bowl of popcorn sat on a nearby end table. Crystal settled beside her.

"Of course he has to take it. It's what he's always wanted—what he's worked for all these years. He'll be producing his own show. How can he turn that down?"

Crystal's heart swelled at the sadness in her sister's eyes. Megs didn't seem to be overreacting for once. Suddenly, Crystal straightened, gasping. "He didn't ask you to go with him."

With another sniffle, Megs set down her bowl and reached for the popcorn. "Oh, no, he wants me to go. He wants me to fly up there with him tomorrow to look at possible places for us to live. He's already scoped out this beautiful town house he wants me to see. Some friend of a friend is subletting it for real cheap." She shrugged. "Well, cheap for New York."

"So, what's the problem?"

"I told him I had to think about it."

"You don't want to leave Atlanta?"

"I—I like it here. I have my friends. My family. My job. I like the paralegal work I do. I really click with everyone at the office. Do you know how rare that is? I don't want to give it up."

"That would be tough. So, you're just going to let him go, then?"

Fresh tears streamed down Megs's face. "I don't know."

"Do you love him?"

She shrugged helplessly. "I thought I did, but now I'm not sure and I have to decide. He's starting the new job in two weeks."

Crystal scooped up a stray piece of popcorn and rolled it in her hand. "But, hon, you don't have to decide by then, do you?"

"He asked me to marry him." The statement brought on a fresh batch of tears.

"That puts a different spin on things."

"This is the biggest decision I've ever had to make. What if I mess up?"

"The Golden Child mess up? Impossible."

"Don't say that. I hate when you say that."

"But it's true. You have a gift for doing the right thing. You don't make mistakes."

"Yes, I do. I don't exactly announce them every time, so you don't notice."

"You don't mess up on the big stuff, though. It's a fact of life that keeps the world stable for us lesser mortals."

"Well, this *is* big stuff."

"Trust yourself. You'll do just fine."

"Or I'll mess up and it'll be *really* bad."

"What's the worst that could happen?"

Megs's eyes rounded as she considered the possibilities. "I could let the love of my life walk away and live the rest of my life regretting it?"

Crystal stilled. "Do you really believe everyone has a true love?"

If possible, Megs's eyes grew even rounder. "Yes, absolutely."

"So…so how do you know when you find your true love?"

"You…just…know. It kind of hits you."

"But you said you weren't sure about Leo. Does that mean he isn't your true love?"

"I have *very* strong feelings for him."

"Feelings that just hit you?"

"Well…when we first met, there was this immediate attraction."

"Love at first sight?"

"Maybe it was more like lust at first sight."

"Is there a difference?"

"Hell if I know. That's what worries me. I could be totally wrong about everything. Things are good with Leo—really good. Maybe this is as good as it gets."

"Do you want to move to New York?"

Megs popped a few kernels into her mouth. She chewed slowly, before finally responding, "Whenever I think about it, my stomach clenches and I break out in this cold sweat."

"That's not good."

"No."

"Well, go with him tomorrow and see what you think. You never know."

Megs's shoulders heaved as she drew in a deep breath. "I guess I could do that. I've never been to New York. I should check it out before making a decision."

"You might really like it."

"Maybe."

"I'd miss you. And Mom and Dad will hate it if you move, especially all the way to New York City."

"They're so tied up in their stuff—Dad's promotion, the new house."

"What is with them and that house?"

"The mausoleum?"

"Yeah, what was wrong with the old house?"

Megs shrugged. "You know Dad always wanted to spoil Mom, get her a beautiful place where she can decorate to her heart's content."

"But it's so…much."

"They can afford it now. It makes them happy."

"Well, I don't get it, but even that big house won't distract them enough to keep them from fretting over you moving to the Big Apple."

"*If* I move."

They were silent a moment, then Megs smiled. "Talking about it helps. Thanks."

"Sure."

"So, what's going on with you?"

Crystal shrugged. "Nothing. Same old, same old."

"I'm always here for you, too, if you ever need it, you know."

Her heart warmed at her sister's offer, but Megs had enough on her plate. It wasn't as though Crystal's problems were life altering. "I know. I think I'll have some of that ice cream, after all."

SMOKE CURLED AROUND the dimly lit room in the Atlanta Country Club, where Sam's father had been a member for decades. The smell of cigars and fine brandy contrasted sharply with the earlier scents from that afternoon at the bar. Even the various conversations of the members scattered about in leather chairs and sofas seemed hushed compared to the clamor of the afternoon.

Sam settled back in his seat. The dark paneled walls and rich mahogany furniture spoke of luxury and wealth, but the club had always been a little too stuffy for his tastes. His father, however, flourished here, secure in his element.

Robert Schaffer set his empty glass down on the end table between them. "So, how's the magazine?"

How many times had he asked that since he'd retired last year and left Sam with the title of CEO? It was a simple question, yet it had so many underlying meanings. It relayed all his father's concerns about whether or not Sam was capable of filling the shoes he had vacated. It was a relentless reminder that his father still held back the controlling shares until Sam could prove himself.

"The magazine's doing well, Dad, as always. We made it into production Friday without a hitch and we had a great brainstorming session on the July issue. You know it's still a great team."

"Of course, of course. I handpicked each one of them. And what about the National Magazine Awards? Think we've got a chance?"

"As good a shot as any of the other finalists. I still want to add that column I told you about. It could clinch it for next year."

"What column?"

Sam tamped down on his frustration. He'd discussed the column in detail with his father on more than one occasion, but his father tended to have memory lapses about Sam's ideas to add some depth to the magazine's upbeat image.

"The one from a woman's perspective." He deliberately left out the details.

Of course he wanted the column to cover the obvious, like what women think about dating and sex, but he also wanted to see the female point of view on harder issues, like job security and worldviews. With all the resistance he'd been experiencing, he'd have to ease his father into that, though.

"You don't want to mess with the formula. We worked hard to get just the right combination of articles, graphics and columns. Our readers, not to mention our advertisers, appreciate that. Don't tamper with success."

"I don't want to tamper with that success. I just want to improve on it."

Taking a moment to focus his thoughts, Sam fingered his empty glass. He and his father had always been in agreement, before the retirement. The longer the company remained in Sam's hands, though, the more it seemed their views of the magazine differed.

He leaned forward. "I just think we can broaden our perspective some. Did you know the number of female subscribers has grown almost twenty percent in the past two quarters?"

Robert waved his hand in dismissal. "Yes, there's always room for improvement. For thirty some years I oversaw the final layout of every page. And I strove to make each issue better than the last, even if that meant throwing out a project and starting again from scratch.''

His father had certainly been known as a perfectionist. Once, at the eleventh hour, Sam had had to have a layout reshot and had rewritten the accompanying article himself, at his father's direction. It had been a harrowing night, but somehow, he'd managed. Surprisingly, he hadn't minded the extra work. He'd trusted his father's judgment and that issue had broken all sales records.

And even though the old man seemed less than supportive of the changes Sam wanted to make, Sam would always value his opinion.

''Best effort every time. I agree,'' Sam said.

A weary sigh escaped his father, and he settled back into the softness of the chair. The grooves of his face seemed etched deeper, the worry lines more pronounced. There had been a time, long ago, when a love for life had lit his eyes and his face had glowed with the vitality of youth.

Before the pain and betrayal of a selfish woman.

Sam shoved the memory back into the safe little compartment in his mind, refusing to revisit the fact that his mother had not only walked out on his father, she'd abandoned her son. The day she'd left, he'd promised himself he'd never allow anyone to hurt him like that again. He'd closed up his heart as tightly as they'd sealed up the box that contained all they had left of her: a gold-plated brush, some photographs and her wedding and engagement rings.

The old feelings of protectiveness gripped him as he glanced at his father. The battle with cancer that had hurried his retirement had taken its toll. Though the best doctors money could buy had assured them he'd beat the disease, the possibility of a recurrence remained.

"You okay, Dad?"

"I'm just a tired old man these days," he said, his eyes closed.

Sam winced inwardly, though he kept his expression passive. His father was only fifty-seven, not old by any standard. Leaning forward, Sam squeezed his father's hand. "Why don't you head home and get some rest? I'll see you next Thursday at the board meeting, if not sooner."

Robert nodded, but remained seated. "God, I'd love to see you win that award."

"*Us* win. It's still your magazine, too. The board will never let you go."

"You'll all be happy to see me go one of these days."

"Not likely."

"New blood is a good thing. You've energized the staff in a way I couldn't have. You've brought the magazine to a whole new level."

"Not me. The staff *you* trained has done a damn good job. It's been a concerted effort. And if we win this award, it's due to all the work you've done in the past to make it the magazine it is today."

Robert stared off into the distance for a moment, then leaned closer. "Tell you what. I'll make you a deal. Do a trial run on this column of yours and we'll see what the numbers do. Get Crystal to write it. She got great reader response from that piece she did for us."

He leaned back and pierced Sam with his clear gaze. ''If the column flies, you'll have your controlling interest. Mind me, that's a big *if.* I can't see any merit in it, myself.''

Sam hesitated for a moment, weighing the merits of cutting a deal with Crystal, torn between fulfilling his vision of the magazine and helping her hook up with Kincaid.

Thanks anyway. I'll figure something out.

And she would. The woman had a stubborn streak a mile wide. If she really wanted Kincaid, she'd stop at nothing until she had him. Would it be so horrible for Sam to help her, and, in doing so, gain the ability to create the magazine in his own vision?

''It's a deal.'' He offered a hand to his father and they shook on it.

''You do something for me, Sam.'' Robert gripped his hand and shifted forward, his gaze piercing. ''You win that award. I don't care what you have to do. This year, next year—however long it takes. You win that award...for all of us.''

Sam swallowed, the weight of his father's request settling heavy on his shoulders. ''I will, Dad. I will.''

3

"CRYSTAL, SAM'S HERE." Megs's voice reached Crystal from a muffled distance.

She groaned softly and twisted away from her sister's insistent prodding. Pillows shifted beneath her. Her hip ground into the carpet.

She cursed softly. "What am I doing on the floor?"

Megs pulled a pillow from her head, and Crystal squinted into the morning light filtering through the maple tree outside her front picture window.

Tossing the pillow back on her, Megs said, "I tried to get you to go to bed, but you fell asleep while we were watching videos."

That was right. She and Megs had finished the night binging on ice cream, popcorn and hot chocolate and watching old home movies their mom had shot. With a wide yawn, she pushed herself into a sitting position. "*Who's* here?"

"Someone who wants to talk to you about your proposition." Sam lounged in one of the oversize faux-leather chairs she'd bought from a consignment shop. His legs looked impossibly long from her vantage point on the floor.

"My proposition?"

"I'll get us some coffee." Megs disappeared into the kitchen.

Feeling inexplicably vulnerable, Crystal hugged one of the big pillows to her chest, while he leaned forward, steepling his fingers. ''I've been thinking about what you said yesterday—about me helping you with a makeover.''

Hope surged through her. ''So, you've reconsidered?''

''Could be.''

''I was thinking. I'd pay you for your time and effort, but I know you don't need the money. Maybe I could do something else for you, like wash all your clothes for the next few weeks.''

''I *was* hoping you'd sweeten the deal, but I had something else in mind.''

The gurgling of the coffeemaker drifted in from the kitchen, along with the tantalizing aroma of coffee. Her stomach rumbled. How she could be hungry after a night of stuffing herself on sweets escaped her.

''Um, I'm not the best in the kitchen, but I do okay,'' she said. ''You want me to cook for you? You like my lasagna. I could make you a week's worth of meals.''

He shook his head.

''Two weeks'?''

''Nope.''

''Clean your house?'' She wrinkled her nose. Housekeeping had never been a priority for her, but this was an unusual situation.

''Nothing quite so menial. I had something else in mind. I was thinking more along the lines of putting your creative talents to use.''

''Creative talents?''

"Your knack for stringing words together. You have an uncanny sense of the written language."

"Oh, no...you're talking about that column again, aren't you?"

"It makes great sense. You want me to make you over. I want you to take on that column. I can't believe we didn't think of this yesterday."

"You were too busy turning me down."

"I'm willing to admit I may have been a little on the hasty side."

"What if I don't want to do the column?"

His shoulders shifted in an easy shrug, the muscles rippling in a fluid motion. "Then I guess I'll have to find someone else. Like you said, there are plenty of female writers out there who'd love the opportunity."

"Then you'll consider a different trade?"

"No. If I can find someone else to write the column, then you can find someone else to do your makeover."

"What makeover?" Megs moved across the room, carrying a tray of steaming mugs, her eyes wide with surprise. "Crystal, you want a makeover?"

Crystal shifted. "Yeah. I don't want people thinking I'm one of the guys anymore."

"I can't believe it." Megs shook her head in disbelief. She set the tray on the low table before the sofa. "I just never thought I'd see the day. We should mark this on the calendar."

Aggravated, Crystal tossed a pillow at her. Megs fended it off. "Hey, I can help you with a makeover."

Crystal glanced away from her sister. Megs was pretty in her own right, with her honey-blond hair and blue eyes, but she had an overall appeal that said "wholesome" as opposed to "sexy." Not that this was a bad thing. Megs had never lacked for male companionship, unlike Crystal who tended to hit dry spells every now and then. Something told Crystal Megs wouldn't understand what she was after, though, especially since she'd never approved of Ron.

"Thanks, sweetie, but you have enough to worry about right now. Besides, Sam's perfectly capable."

Nodding silently, Megs handed her one of the mugs. "Coffee?" she asked, turning to Sam.

"Thanks." He took the offered mug, cradling it in his big hands. His eyes narrowed and his eyebrows drew together as he turned back to Crystal. "I'll do your makeover, if you'll do the column."

A feeling of unease crept over her. "What if the column stinks? What if I can't deliver what you want?"

He waved his hand in dismissal. "That won't happen."

Tiny dust motes swirled in the sunlight as she stirred sugar into her coffee. "I don't want you to feel obligated to print whatever tripe I might spit out."

"Let me worry about that. Give it your best shot. *I* know you can do it."

Megs sighed and sat back on her heels, sipping silently from her mug. She nodded encouragingly at Crystal. "I'm with Sam. You're destined for greater things."

Ignoring her, Crystal addressed Sam, "Let me get this straight. You'll turn me into a hot sex goddess and in return, all I have to do is prove to you that I can't write this column of yours."

"All you have to do is give the column your best shot."

She blew on her coffee, then took a tentative sip. The liquid ran strong and sweet down her throat. Could she write his column? She *would* have to put forward her best effort, but somehow the thought of Sam rejecting her work struck her as worse than all the rejections she'd had in the past.

"I don't know," she said.

His expression, as usual, remained unreadable. "It's your choice."

He set down his coffee and started to rise.

"Wait." Crystal rose to her knees, the memory of Ron smiling down at her vivid in her mind. She hesitated a long moment, then put down her cup. She rose, then covered the few steps to stand before Sam.

Drawing up straight, she looked him in the eye. "How would we make sure this makeover sticks? Maybe we need some kind of stipulation."

"What do you mean?"

"What would keep me from backsliding into my not-so-sexy ways? You see, I don't want this to be just a surface makeover. If I'm going to stand any chance at making it into this calendar, I can't just look sexy. I have to *be* sexy. And you know what a long shot that is."

She laughed a short, tense little laugh that sounded insecure, even to her own ears. "It's going to be really hard for me follow your lead in this case. This is unknown territory for me. You'll need to tell me what to do and how to do it. We can't pull this off unless I follow your directions to a T. And you know

I'm not always good at that, so you'll need to be firm with me. You need to be...you know...controlling."

"Controlling?"

"Yes, you need to make sure I do whatever you say. I trust you completely, Sam. I'll put myself into your care. It's essential that you direct my life for the duration of this project. It's the only way I can make this transformation. I'll..." She frowned, waving her fingers as though trying to draw the right word to her. "I'll...submit to you."

Sam swallowed. The intensity of her gaze sent heat spiraling from his gut outward. He stared at her, dazed. "Submit to me?"

She laughed. "Well, you know, not in a sexual sense, but other than that, yes, completely."

Silence stretched between them. He licked his suddenly dry lips. She trusted him. And she should. Of course she had to place a limitation on such a stipulation.

She had been his friend and confidante for almost as long as he remembered. Lost in her gaze, he couldn't deny her. Even if it killed him.

If she wanted him to transform her, then he'd stop at nothing until he'd made her into the sex goddess she meant to be. Not that it would be any hard feat. He had only to help her recognize what was already there.

What might it be like to have her respond to his every request? How would he keep those requests targeted on their goal and not let them veer off into his own fantasies? Of course, she'd specified that they'd draw the line there, but how could he keep his imagination from crossing that fine line? The woman was going to be more of a distraction than he bargained for.

She lifted her chin and stuck out her hand, her gaze clear and intent. "Deal?"

His stomach clenched as he gripped her hand and a feeling of foreboding stole over him. "Deal."

"HERE, THIS IS THE LAST ONE." Loni Berch, the magazine's makeup artist, snapped her gum as she secured a hot roller in Crystal's hair later that morning, nestling it beside its comrades.

Sam paced along the narrow aisle behind the salon chair, which was crowded into one end of the magazine's photography studio. He inhaled the sharp scents of nail polish and hair spray and rolled his shoulders in an effort to relax. He felt caged, his body drawn as taut as a bow.

Maybe asking Loni to come in on a Sunday hadn't been the best idea, but he had wanted to get this makeover nonsense done with as soon as possible. And Loni, in spite of her gum smacking and big hair, was the best makeup artist he'd ever dealt with, versatile enough to handle not only Crystal's makeup but her pedicure, manicure and hair, as well.

A wide grin split Crystal's face as she turned her head from side to side, assessing the mass of curlers. "First all that fuss over painting my fingernails and toenails, now this. A girl sure has to go through a lot of silliness to get to being a sex goddess."

"When I am done with you—" Loni's own lacquered nails shone as she tilted Crystal's chin up and flourished a puffy brush "—you won't feel the least bit silly, hon. In fact, my guess is you'll take one look and see the provocative beauty you were meant to be.''

Sam cursed softly and continued pacing as Loni bent over her charge, clucking like a mother hen, every now and then snapping her gum. ''Now for your makeup.''

''Explain exactly what you're doing, so she can recreate it later on her own,'' he said, clenching his fists.

Why Crystal wanted to tarnish her natural beauty was beyond him. She couldn't have thought this through. The woman was more impulsive than was good for her. But he'd made a deal. And he meant to see this to the dismal end, then claim his controlling interest at the first opportunity.

For what seemed an agonizingly long time, Loni smacked and chewed, brushed and dabbed, patted and smudged, all the while keeping up a steady dialogue that seemed to have Crystal entranced.

Sam peered over Loni's shoulder. She had done a fair job of enhancing Crystal's features, but the effect needed to be more dramatic if Crystal meant to make it into that calendar. ''Let's try another coat of mascara and darker lipstick. And see what you can do to accent those high cheekbones.''

With a curt nod, Loni set to work again. After what seemed ages, she stepped back and Crystal leaned forward, blinking at her reflection. ''Well, would you look at that? I have eyelashes.''

''It's amazing what a little mascara can do. Now, hold still.'' With her own blond curls bobbing, Loni finished with a dab of powder to Crystal's nose. Smiling, she straightened and rubbed her hands together,

her eyes bright with anticipation. ''Now, let's see about your hair.''

Using the same efficient movements, she whisked the rollers one by one from the blond locks. ''Your hair is perfect. Look how it takes the curl.''

''That's extraordinary.'' Crystal pulled on a strand, straightening it, then letting it bounce back into place.

A frown creased Loni's forehead. ''How a girl as pretty as you could have gone this long without ever playing dress up is beyond me. If I had your hair, I'd be wearing it different every day.''

Crystal's gaze met Sam's in the mirror, then slid away. ''It just never seemed important before.''

''Must be a man.''

''I think you can manage all this with a little less conversation.'' Sam frowned at Loni.

She merely rolled her eyes, then gestured to Crystal. ''Lean forward and finger comb it.''

She did as Loni asked. When she was through, Loni motioned again with her hands. ''Now, flip your head up and let it all fall back.''

The thick mass flew up, then back, settling around Crystal's shoulders in a curtain of platinum swirls as she straightened. Light from an overhead fixture danced across the surface, adding luster and shine. Her face seemed softer, more open.

Sam stood rooted for a moment, his heart thumping. She was stunning. Unable to stop himself, he moved behind her and sank his fingers into the silky depths, breathing deeply of her floral-scented shampoo. Silky strands cascaded over his fingers as he scooped handfuls of the shimmering curls to the crown of her head.

"How about something like this?" he asked.

Loni puckered her lips. "Yes, I like it piled up like that, loose, but flowing. What do you say, Crystal?"

Crystal caught his eye in the mirror. "Whatever Sam wants. He's the boss."

Her words sent a wave of excitement rolling over him. It had been a secret fantasy that had haunted him for years—to have her completely in his control, to dress her up if he wanted to, undress her if he wanted to…play with her, if he wanted to.

I'll…submit to you.

Of course, he'd never take advantage of their pact. It would be insane to get involved with her while she pursued another man. Not that their relationship had ever taken on any sexual undertones.

But a guy couldn't help fantasizing.

"Let me see." Loni moved beside Sam, and he reluctantly loosened his hold, letting the soft tendrils slip over his hands as he withdrew them. After a few moments of tucking, smacking and pinning, Loni stepped back, a satisfied smile gracing her face.

This time, Sam's heart stopped. The fall of curls, the makeup accenting her long lashes and full lips and the awe-filled look in her eyes, all formed a picture so poignantly beautiful that all he could do was stare and try to etch every line, every curve of her face into his memory. Not even in his wildest fantasies had he imagined such a transformation.

"You clean up nice, hon. Don't you think, Sam?" Loni's matter-of-fact tone yanked him back to earth.

He straightened, carefully concealing his reaction. "That'll do."

"Oh, no it won't." Crystal surged to her feet, tear-ing off the protective wrap Loni had placed over her top. "It won't do at all."

"And why not?" he asked.

"Well..." She spread her arms wide. "The rest of me doesn't match."

His gaze swept her rumpled jeans and T-shirt. *Damn.* She was right. They'd only just begun this makeover.

The loud smack of Loni's gum cracked through the air. "Looks like you two get to do some clothes shopping."

Crystal sighed and turned to him. "We might as well get it over with now. You ready?"

A vision of this new Crystal standing before him in a slinky black dress revealing her every curve and hollow flashed through his mind.

Dress her up if he wanted to...

He lifted his chin and drew a deep breath to steady the pounding of his heart. "Let's do it."

THEY'D DONE IT. Sam reached for the last garment bag as Crystal thanked the beaming sales clerk later that afternoon. She'd probably come close to maxing out that new credit card of hers. A clock on the wall showed the afternoon was waning.

Three hours.

Three hours in more trendy mall shops than he could keep track of. Three hours of sorting through dresses and skirts and oh-so-small tops, visualizing each low-cut neckline, high-cut hem and form-hugging fit on her hot little body.

Three hours of agonizing, waiting, imagining her peeling off her clothes, shimmying into the sleek new outfits, then smoothing the silky fabrics over her curves.

Three hours of sitting passively by as she teetered out on spike heels, then pivoted shyly to see all angles in the three-way mirror, while he tried not to notice how she looked ten times sexier than his wildest fantasy.

And somehow he'd kept his libido in check the entire time. Thank God it was over. He stepped back and held the shop door open for her, doing his best not to notice the bold curve of her breasts, revealed by the low cut of her new top or the way her short skirt just hugged her ass, skimming the firm swells of her buttocks.

"We've only got about an hour. We'd better hurry."

"An hour for what?" When had she learned to walk on those heels? He hurried after her.

She cocked her head, without slowing her pace. "Secret Temptations."

"What?" Had she read his mind?

"This way. Secret Temptations, that new lingerie shop. I saw it on the way in. This is where I should have come yesterday. They just opened this Northpoint branch. Their commercials are pretty upbeat. Hopefully they won't have any of those snooty saleswomen."

"Lingerie shop?"

"Well, yes. It *is* a lingerie calendar."

Heat raced through him. "You want me to help you shop for lingerie?"

"Of course. This is where I *really* need your input. That was just the warm-up back there. This is the tough part. I have no idea what half the stuff in there is.'' She looped her arm through his and nodded at the storefront.

A wide window brazenly displayed an assortment of lingerie made of black leather and lace. A vision of Crystal wearing the skimpy apparel flashed through his mind. His groin tightened.

How the hell was he supposed to keep his libido in check through *this?*

''Come on.'' She tugged on his arm. ''I can't go in there alone. It wreaks havoc on my ego. I'm counting on your moral support.''

Too bad he had such a loose grip on his morals at the moment. Nonetheless, he let her steer him inside. The tinkle of the door sounded like an alarm in his head. A faint scent of lavender laced the air as soft lights played over the colorful interior.

''Okay, now what?'' Crystal looked up at him, her arm still threaded through his, her eyes wide and so blue he thought he might drown in them.

His gaze skimmed over the soft rise and fall of her breasts as she stood pressed to his side. She'd always kept her body hidden under loose clothes, but that had never fooled him. He'd been constantly aware of her sleek, firm figure. Now, seeing her curves out in plain sight for anyone to view was most disconcerting.

He blinked and focused on her face. ''Well, do you have any preference?''

''This is all Greek to me. I'm normally a boxers and T-shirt kind of girl. Besides, I was hoping you could tell me. You're calling the shots.''

For some strange reason, the image of her in boxers sent an erotic thrill through him. He glanced around.

"I have an idea. Let's start with something you're familiar with, then ease you into the rest."

She followed his gaze to a wall displaying silk boxers in a rainbow of gem tones. "Okay, that might work."

"Good afternoon," a young woman with flaming red hair greeted them.

Sam nodded, but Crystal stiffened beside him. He patted her hand reassuringly. "Afternoon. Is it okay if we just look around?"

"Sure. My name's Bridget. I'll be putting out some of our new stock. We have a special section of erotic wear. It was all designed by Norma Craig, our owner here at Secret Temptations. She's a hoot. I'd be happy to show you the line if you're interested."

"Maybe a little later," Crystal said, and it was Sam's turn to tense.

"Let me know if you need anything. The dressing rooms are there, past that display of teddies." Bridget pointed.

"Thank you," Sam and Crystal spoke in unison as the woman turned away.

"Okay…boxers." He gripped her hand, then led her to the wall display. Reaching out, he took hold of one of the garments. The fabric ran smooth and satiny between his fingers as he lifted the boxers to hold in front of her. "Why don't you try these? I really like this emerald with your coloring."

She nodded and reached tentatively to touch the fabric. "Whatever you say. And for on top?"

An assortment of silk tank tops flanked the boxers. He pulled down one in a matching shade. "This'll do."

"I'll try these on, but we still need to pick out some other things." She waved toward the store in general. "I don't know, Sam. Maybe some of the sexier items? I'm not so sure about that erotic wear, but maybe we should work our way up to that."

His throat constricted. "I don't think you'll need that for the calendar."

"No, but I'm cultivating passion here. I need to feel as sexy as possible, don't I? If I can capture that by wearing something really naughty, maybe I can project that feeling when I'm posing for Ron in something a little less naughty."

If Sam had any say, the only nightwear Ron would see her in would be flannel pajamas. Oversize flannel pajamas. But surely she would be sexy even in those. "Let's see what we can find here."

He turned to a table covered with stacks of something made of a gauzy fabric. He lifted one garment, unfolding a peach-colored teddy made of almost translucent fibers. God, she'd be incredible in it. His blood thrummed in his ears as he gazed at the thin straps and lacy bodice.

"Wow." Crystal's voice came from directly beside him. The heat of her body pressed into his side. "That's really sexy, isn't it?"

He nodded mutely.

"So…I guess I should try it on."

"Right." He draped the garment over her arm, then moved stiffly to the next table.

She poked at the soft piles covering its surface, then gingerly lifted a pair of panties. She twisted them to reveal a thong back. "I can't imagine anyone being comfortable in these."

"You won't know until you try them."

"You find them sexy?"

"Very." In fact, he was so aroused at the moment, walking might be a problem.

"Okay. I don't think I can try on any of the panties, but I'll go ahead and buy some." She eyed the scanty garment. "They should fit. I should find a matching bra, though. Don't you think?"

He thought it was getting very warm in there, but nodded. "Definitely."

After adding the thong to the stack draped over her arm, she sorted through the bras arranged on a fixture beside the panties. She held one up, examining it closely.

"This is very…low cut." She pressed it to her front. "I think this is my size, but will it cover my nipples?"

He closed his eyes and drew a deep breath, trying desperately to squelch the vision of her rosy nipples, straining within the confines of the bra. "The cut is part of the style. It's meant to tease."

"Oh." She blinked, but added the item to her stack, then turned and headed for a fixture on the next aisle. "What next? What are these?"

He picked out one of the leather-and-lace garments, holding it up for her to see. "These are called merry widows."

"Okay." She leaned away from the table as if one of the garments might attack her.

"Let's try a black one," he said. "The contrast with your light coloring will be devastating."

"Devastating?" She laughed. "It's hard for me to think of myself as devastating."

"Sweetheart, get used to it. With this makeover, you'll be the most devastating woman around. You'll have men falling at your feet."

"I only want one man."

The statement was like a cold slap in his face. He stood stunned for a moment. What an idiot he was. How could he have forgotten?

"Well, of course, but that won't keep the rest from wanting you." He kept his voice light, neutral.

She cocked her head and gazed at him. "You're very good for my ego. I knew I needed you here with me."

"Anytime." Honestly, he felt anything but helpful at that moment. The urge to punch something nearly overwhelmed him. Why the hell had he agreed to this?

The column. He wasn't likely ever to have Crystal for himself, but the column—and the controlling interest, not to mention the National Magazine Awards—were certainly attainable now that he had her cooperation. First, though, he had to pay the price.

"Maybe I should go ahead and try these on?" She looked to him, her eyebrows arched in question.

"Sure." He walked with her to the dressing room.

"I don't see that saleswoman, but I guess it's okay to go in."

"I'll wait for you here." He gestured to a small area, containing a love seat and a pair of cushioned chairs. It was a fancy enough setting for a condemned man.

4

CRYSTAL SHIFTED THE CLOTHES on her arm. Unease filled her. Entering the dressing room alone in the last few shops hadn't been as bad as her experience yesterday, but now she felt intimidated all over again. "What if I...um, have any trouble?"

Sam hesitated, then settled himself firmly in one of the chairs. He grabbed a magazine from a nearby table before answering, "If you can't manage on your own, let me know and I'll get one of the salesgirls to help. Just start with the boxers. You'll be fine."

"Right." She could do this. It wasn't as if she didn't dress herself every day. She shouldn't let a couple of scraps of silk get the better of her.

Drawing a deep breath, she entered the dressing room. It was surprisingly spacious, with a padded red chair in one corner. She hung the clothes on a hook, then peered at her reflection.

Curls framed her face and brushed the nape of her neck. Her eyes seemed huge and somehow bluer, her lips fuller. And her body...she turned sideways to survey the form-hugging outfit. She'd never thought of herself as having curves, but suddenly she seemed to have them and in all the right places.

Was that really her?

Her blood warmed. What would Ron think of her

now? Not a trace of the old Crystal remained. Would he even recognize her? Would he possibly find her attractive?

Excitement raced up her spine. Quickly, she shed the top and skirt, then slipped off her bra. She hesitated over her own cotton panties. She'd fished them out from the bottom of her drawer. They were the skimpiest pair she owned. She should be able to try on most of these things over them.

"Okay, you first." She addressed the silk boxers.

Slipping into them was a cinch and the tank top wasn't any problem, either. Her spirits lifted. She moved and the soft fabric brushed over her hips and breasts. She turned before the mirror. They seemed to fit okay.

"That wasn't so hard."

After opening the dressing-room door, she struck a dramatic pose and waited for Sam to glance up from his magazine. His gaze swept over her, sending unprecedented shivers of awareness through her. Heat prickled along her spine and settled low in her belly.

She stilled as his gaze locked with hers. Some dark emotion flickered in his green depths, warming her blood. Then he straightened and his face took on the same calm expression he always wore. Had she imagined it or had that been desire in his eyes? She shook her head. She was losing it.

He rose, then came to lean nonchalantly against the doorjamb. "The boxers look good. That's a great color on you. They're actually quite sexy. I like the way the fabric moves over your body. How does it feel?"

Her heart thudded softly at his nearness. Funny,

she'd never noticed before how nice he smelled. Like fresh air and a familiar muskiness.

That's right—she'd borrowed an old sweater of his once and it had smelled like him. She still had it. It was one of her favorites, though his scent had long since faded from it.

His eyebrows rose, calling her back to their conversation. She shrugged in answer to his question and the silk whispered over her like a caress. "It's soft. I like it."

"Ready for the teddy?" His voice melted over her like warm honey. There was something different in his tone, something...enticing.

She blinked, banishing the thought. Her imagination was running wild, trying to make him into some mystery man.

This was Sam. *He* hadn't gone through any transformation. He was still her friend and confidante, as reliable and trustworthy as ever.

"Sure." She glanced beyond him to where several other customers milled around a sale table. "How am I supposed to get your opinion on the rest? I can't exactly model in front of the whole world."

Straightening, he pushed away from the door, his jaw set. "No, you don't have to model for me. And you don't really need my opinion. You can decide what you like without me."

Frustration welled up inside her. "But you're the guy here. I need to know what *you* think is sexy." She gripped his arm, then laughed. "Maybe you could just come take a peek every now and then. I promise not to jump you or anything, if that's what you're worried about."

"And you trust *me* not to jump you?"

The serious tone of his voice sent surprise swirling through her. "I told you this morning. I trust you completely, Sam."

"Maybe you shouldn't."

"I trust you with my life."

His gaze raked over her and, to her surprise, her nipples hardened against the thin fabric.

"Do you trust me with your virtue?" he asked.

She blinked, stunned. "Virtue? There's certainly none of that to worry about."

Then she laughed and teased in a singsong voice, "So, you think I'm sexy."

He leaned in, so close that his nose nearly brushed hers. "I think I'm a man and you're a woman asking me to view you in your dressing room, where you'll be slipping into lingerie designed specifically to entice. You have to know that just the thought of it has me so turned on I can hardly see straight."

"Oh."

Heat rushed to her cheeks. She swallowed. All these years she'd been dying to crack that calm exterior of his. Somehow, she hadn't quite imagined it would happen like this, though.

He was turned on. By her. The thought sent a shiver of excitement and wonder through her. She *did* have what it took. If she could turn on Sam—who'd *never* had a sexy thought about her—surely she'd have a chance with Ron.

"I'll just wait for you over here." He started to move away, but she grabbed him.

"How will I know what looks good?"

"Trust me. It's *all* going to look good. Decide by

how each outfit makes you feel. If it makes you feel sexy, I promise you're going to look sexy in it."

"Okay."

He blew out a breath. "Good. Just let me know if you need me."

He retreated to his seat and she closed herself in again with the lingerie. Forcing her resolve, she lifted the black leather-and-lace merry widow. It was only a piece of clothing—nothing to be intimidated by.

A zipper ran down the front, embedded in leather panels. She shimmied into the garment, gasping as she noted the strategic placement of the lace. "Oh, my, I see why the widow is merry."

Drawing a deep breath, she slipped the zipper upward. Inch by inch, the leather panels drew together and the garment molded to her body. When she reached her breasts, the tab slowed, then stuck.

"Maybe this is the wrong size," she murmured and gave the zipper a yank. It traveled the rest of the way and she turned to the mirror.

Heat again flooded her cheeks, bringing a rosy glow. She just couldn't get used to having all these curves. Her breasts swelled over the cups, the pink flush of her areolae just visible through the lace. She turned and the fabric brushed over her, hardening her nipples.

She drew a deeper breath. Though her breasts remained in the cups, her nipples rubbed teasingly against the lace. Waves of heat washed over her. Her sex pulsed.

This wouldn't do. Biting her lip, she placed her hands over the cups and squeezed her breasts. The sexual ache only intensified.

What would Ron say if he could see her now? With luck, he'd be speechless. She closed her eyes.

His gaze swept her up then down, as he closed the distance between them. He traced her cheek, then kissed her long and hard, his tongue both tantalizing and demanding. His hands skimmed over her leather-and-lace-clad body, sending heat rippling through her. He kissed his way along her neck, while he thumbed her nipple through the lace.

She rolled her head and bit back a moan. His mouth traveled down past her collarbone and he pinched the hardened peak. The warmth of his breath fanned over her breast, just before he took her into his hot mouth, lace and all. The pleasure was so intense, she couldn't hold back a moan.

He drew hard on her breast, eliciting a second moan that started deep in her throat, then crescendoed as it burst from her lips. Desire curled through her and she pressed her body to his and ran her fingers through his sand-colored hair.

Sand-colored hair? Her body shivered as her fantasy man morphed into Sam. Surprise and a forbidden thrill raced through her.

He pushed the lace aside and teased her nipple with his teeth, sliding one hand down to cup her sex. He caressed her through her panties, his movements steady and sure. Another uncontrolled moan tore from her and she ground against him as tension coiled through her.

He slid his hand beneath the elastic, then stroked her swollen flesh. He knew exactly how to touch her—the right pressure to apply. When he slipped his fin-

gers inside her slick entrance, she thought she might die of ecstasy.

Another moan escaped her as he withdrew to spread her liquid heat over her clit. He caressed her in little circles, until her hips moved and the fire inside her built to an impossible level.

"Oh, that feels so good." She cried out, as her body stiffened in release, then she sank into him, nuzzling his neck and breathing in his scent. He smelled of fresh air and a faint muskiness that curled around her like a favorite sweater, a very familiar sweater...

A rapping on the dressing-room door jolted her from her fantasy. "Crystal, is everything okay in there? You sound...you sound hurt."

The deep rumble of Sam's voice through the door sent heat swirling in the pit of her stomach. "No...I'm fine. I'll be out shortly."

Drawing a calming breath, she willed her heart to a steady beat. What had made her fantasize about Sam? Her earlier conversation with him was somehow mixing with her daydream of Ron.

So she liked Sam's scent. It made sense she'd seek out the familiar when everything about her was so different now. Still, a secret excitement swept through her at the thought of opening the door.

She turned again to the mirror. Her reflection showed her flushed face and heaving breasts. A feeling of dismay washed over her. There was a fine line between sexy and slutty. And the latter would never get her a spot in that calendar.

Was the merry widow too much?

Should she get Sam's opinion?

The thought set her nerves on end. Of course she

couldn't show him. He'd already warned her about that. Would he be able to tell how aroused she'd become, just by putting on one little outfit?

Would he read in her eyes the new thoughts she was entertaining on his behalf?

She turned away from the mirror and bumped into the chair. "Shit."

"Crystal?"

"I'm fine. Give me a minute."

Maybe the teddy wouldn't be so evocative. That was what he had wanted her to try on next. She grabbed the zipper pull on the merry widow and yanked. The tab moved down about a quarter of an inch, then stopped.

"Oh, come on. Don't do this now."

She tugged up on it, then down again, but it refused to budge. Again, she repeated the procedure, then a third time, without success.

She groaned in frustration. "No. This can't happen."

Alarm raced up her spine. She should have known something like this would happen. This was why she hated shopping. Nothing ever went right.

She was stuck in the merry widow.

"Crystal? Are you sure everything's okay? You've been in there a long time, honey."

"I'm..." She tugged again to no avail. "I'm having a little problem."

He jiggled the doorknob. "You need some help?"

The thought of him helping her set off a flurry of butterflies in her stomach. "I...don't know."

"I'll go get someone."

"No."

The memory of the snooty saleswoman from yesterday flickered in her mind. Wouldn't she get a kick out of seeing Crystal stuck like this? Would Bridget, the salesclerk here, act in the same manner?

"It's too embarrassing." She closed her eyes on the evident anxiety in her voice.

He jiggled the knob again.

She gave the zipper pull one more futile tug, silently begging it to move. It remained fast.

"Shit."

What else could she do? She couldn't stay trapped in the merry widow forever.

Biting her bottom lip, she opened the door.

Sam peered cautiously inside, drawing a sharp breath at the sight of her. Heat slammed through him. He opened his mouth to speak, but found no words. "Hubba, hubba" just didn't seem to cut it.

"Close the door." She motioned with her hand. "You're just going to have to come in." Her eyes widened and a note of panic tinged her words, snapping him partly out of his trance. "I'm stuck."

"What?" He forced his gaze to her eyes.

"My zipper..." She tugged at the culprit. "It just...won't move."

He swallowed hard, stepped inside, then closed the door and forced himself not to notice the enticing swell of her breasts, or the way the garment barely contained their rosy tips. Taking a step closer, he breathed deeply of her scent. He'd know it anywhere—her floral shampoo mixed with her own unique essence.

Only her scent seemed somehow stronger, more enticing than before.

"Okay, let's see." He slipped his fingers inside her bodice to steady the zipper, while he tugged with his other hand. His knuckles sank into the softness of her breast as he worked at the zipper. It remained stuck. She moaned softly and closed her eyes.

"Did I hurt you?" he asked, his heart thudding.

She shook her head. "No. Try not to shift the bodice so much, though."

He frowned, unable to keep his gaze from the lacy cups. Her nipples pressed against the fabric, clearly visible and straining to be touched. He bit back a moan of his own.

Damn, he had to get her out of this so he could make a hasty escape. He couldn't take much more of this. The woman was killing him.

"Okay, don't panic. We'll get you free." He grasped the top of the zipper and tugged again.

This time, it moved another fraction of an inch. "I think I'm getting it."

"Oh, good." She sounded breathless.

Wriggling the tab from side to side, he managed another quarter of an inch. She moaned again and he stopped, the sound arousing him beyond reason. "Crystal, are you sure I'm not hurting you?"

Again she shook her head. Then she opened her eyes and looked at him, desire swimming in her blue depths. "It's just that I have very sensitive nipples and every time the lace rubs across them..."

He cursed under his breath as his cock went hard as a rock. His heart thudded. He stood for a moment mesmerized. She was gazing at him with that look—the look that said he was that special someone.

"I'll...I'll try not to rub them," he stammered.

A slow smile spread across her lips, the sexiest damn smile he'd ever seen. "So, what do think?"

He thought he was going to die if he couldn't tear this thing off her, then pump himself inside her until they both screamed in ecstasy.

"About what?"

"About the merry widow. Is it sexy?"

"Hell yes."

"Not slutty?" Her forehead puckered in worry.

He tipped up her chin, so he could gaze into her eyes. "*You* could never look slutty."

"But I look sexy?"

As if of its own volition, his thumb stroked her full bottom lip. "Oh, yeah."

Her tongue flicked out and darted across his thumb, then she laughed a short, nervous laugh. "I'm sorry. I was just thinking about how I like the way you smell and I wondered how you tasted."

The breath left his body. He stared at her, no coherent words forming in his head.

"Remember that old sweater of yours I borrowed and never returned? It smelled like you for a long time and I used to wrap myself in it to feel warm and safe."

Nothing else she could have said would have aroused him more. He bit the inside of his cheek, fighting the overpowering urge to devour her mouth with his. "Sweetheart, you shouldn't tell me these things. I don't think you should be feeling so safe with me, right this minute."

Her gaze held his for a long moment. For one crazy second he let himself believe the desire in her eyes was all directed toward him.

She cocked her head. "I still trust you, Sam."

It seemed all the saliva drained from his mouth. He had to get her out of the merry widow, so he could beat a hasty retreat. "Let's try this again, shall we? Here, you hold the top."

"Like this?"

"Right. And I'll get the bottom. Now, this rocking seemed to work." By moving the tab back and forth, he finally got it to give a little more, then, to his profound relief, it slid down the rest of the way.

"Thanks." She beamed up at him and he tore his gaze from the creamy expanse of flesh exposed by the open zipper.

"I'd better go."

"Wait." Crystal reached for Sam. Confusion and unfulfilled need swirled through her in a most disconcerting fashion.

She refused to ponder why, but the thought of him walking out that door sent an almost desperate ache through her. She *wanted* him with her. "You might as well stay, since you're here."

He stared at her in disbelief. "I don't know. That's a really bad idea."

Before she could analyze her actions, she led him to the red cushioned chair. "You can face the other way when I'm dressing. Sit and get comfy. Now, you wanted me to try the teddy, right?"

He made no response, other than to nod, his gaze fixed on hers. She swallowed, feeling as if she stood in the spotlight. Even seated, he seemed suddenly bigger, taking up much of the room with his presence, shrinking what had been an adequate space to an area of intimacy.

Slowly, he pivoted in the chair. When he safely faced the wall, she relaxed and glanced down. Heat shot through her at the sight of the gaping front of the merry widow. Her hands slightly trembling, she fingered the peach teddy.

"Okay," she said, a small tremor in her voice, "This looks pretty harmless. Straps over the arms, lace bodice in front. And…snaps…down there."

Heat flamed again in her cheeks at the thought of the purpose of those snaps. She hesitated a moment, before turning her back to Sam to slip off the merry widow, even though he still faced the wall. No doubt he'd seen scores of naked women before and surely she was nothing to write home about, but there was no sense taking any chances.

Still, those butterflies again took flight.

She drew a deep breath and gave herself a mental shake. She needed to focus. If she was going to pose for that calendar, she had to get over her shyness.

Without looking in his direction, she took the teddy from the hook, then stepped into it. The fabric floated over her, nestling against her body like a soft mist. With a start, she realized her every curve showed clearly through the translucent fabric.

Swallowing, she turned again to the mirror. Heat prickled her skin. With a little difficulty, she secured the row of tiny buttons down the front. The bodice cupped her breasts, her nipples once more peering through lace. The rest of the garment caressed her body as she moved, shimmering with an otherworldly effect.

In this, she *did* have an ethereal beauty.

In spite of her nerves, a smile curved her lips as

she turned to him. ‘‘Okay, you can look. I feel like a fairy princess.’’

‘‘A nymph is more like it.’’ His voice carried a hoarseness that struck a chord deep inside her.

Feeling aroused and powerful, she moved in front of him. With each step, the teddy shifted over her, caressing her. She swayed slightly in front of him, liking the feel of the lace on her skin—skin that had never felt more sensitized. ‘‘So, you like this? You think it's sexy?’’

His hand shot out and clamped around her hip, halting her. ‘‘Damn it, Crystal. Don't tease. Yes, it's sexy.’’

She drew back, suddenly contrite and shocked at her own behavior. She, the woman who didn't even know how to flirt, had just teased him. What was happening to her? ‘‘I'm sorry. I didn't mean to—’’

‘‘Try something else.’’ He waved her away. ‘‘Let's get through this.’’

What *had* gotten into her? She hadn't meant to tease him. It was a surprise that he actually found her attractive and it was a heady feeling to have him react so strongly, but this couldn't be easy for him.

Slowly, she rose, then moved back to the hook. ‘‘What would you like to see next?’’

‘‘Put on the bra and panties.’’

‘‘Okay.’’

He turned back around and she drew a deep breath. The trembling in her fingers increased, making it difficult to grip the slick fabric. She fumbled with the tiny buttons on the teddy. ‘‘Damn.’’

‘‘What's wrong?’’ He turned toward her.

‘‘Nothing.’’ She focused on the buttons, her frustration building. Did they have to be so small? Her nerves got the better of her and she swore again as the stupid buttonholes eluded her. "This is why I hate this. I can't even undress myself."

He closed his eyes for a moment, then pushed up from the chair. The room seemed to shrink even more, with him standing so close again. His knuckles brushed her breasts as he worked the first button free and her pulse quickened.

"I'm sorry," she said. "I really didn't mean to tease you. I'm just not good at this kind of thing. I've always been so awkward around men. You know, never knowing the right thing to say or do."

The thought drifted through her mind that she'd never before been like that with him. It was as if she'd worn blinders in the past and was now finally seeing him not as a friend but as a man. The realization both astounded and bewildered her.

She was sexually attracted to Sam. Where this had come from, she couldn't say, but wicked delight seeped over her as he slipped the second button free.

I'll...submit to you.

What *would* it be like to submit to him on a sexual level?

He remained silent, continuing on to the next button. When he'd finished, he straightened and his gaze met hers. That same dark emotion she'd thought she'd seen earlier shimmered in his eyes. She held her breath. It *was* desire. He *did* feel this insane sexual pull.

He slipped one finger under the shoulder strap, then raised his eyebrows in question. She swallowed and nodded. Carefully, his gaze never leaving hers, he slipped the straps from her shoulders, skimmed the garment down her body, then off her feet, kneeling as she stepped out of it. Only then did his gaze travel over her, passing up her thighs, her hips, her breasts. She held her breath and let him look his fill as tremors of excitement rippled through her.

"We'll take this, as well as the boxers and tank top," he said, as he rose again to his full height.

"And the merry widow?"

"It's lethal. We'll get one with a good zipper."

"Whatever you say, Sam." How many women had uttered those exact words to him?

I'll…submit to you.

She stood beside him, acutely aware of her nakedness and the warmth of his body, yet, in spite of the heated look in his eyes, she felt safe and secure with him. Protected.

How would he react if she suggested they remove the barrier on her stipulation?

He slipped the thong off the hook.

"Oh, I wasn't going to try that on." She plucked at her cotton panties. "Health issues."

"So, we'll buy them. I need to see you in them. You want my opinion, don't you?"

"Sure."

She hesitated a moment. His scent curled around her, evoking the memory of her fantasy of him. What would he say if she told him she'd dreamed of him touching her, putting his mouth on her?

His gaze again slid slowly up her body, lingering at her breasts, before reaching her eyes. "Crystal, did you mean what you said this morning?"

"About the stipulation?"

I'll...submit to you.

He nodded and she closed her eyes. When she had insisted earlier on that stipulation and the fact that it wasn't meant in a sexual sense, she hadn't been feeling so...so drawn to him. But their deal, and especially her stipulation, could have very sexual implications. The thought sent her into a tailspin of further confusion.

And need.

Slowly, she nodded.

"Then you're ready to do as I ask?"

Heat shimmered along her every nerve ending. Again, she nodded.

"Take off your panties."

The soft tone of his voice released the last vestiges of her self-consciousness. With a boldness she never knew she had, she slipped off her panties. Drawing a deep breath, she straightened and stood naked before him.

His gaze swept her from head to toe, sending an intense ripple of desire through her. For one heated moment, his eyes met hers, then he dropped to his knees before her.

He held the thong as she stepped into it. He drew the garment up her legs, then settled it over her hips. The brush of his fingertips sent a thrill along her skin. She reached for the bra, but he took it from her, helping her into it as well. When he fastened the front clasp, his knuckles again brushed her breasts and his breath fanned her chest.

"I've never had anyone dress me before."

"Well." He smiled that rare smile of his. "I've never gotten a woman *into* her lingerie before."

"See? I'm helping you to have new experiences. Widening your horizons."

He didn't laugh as she had hoped, but fussed over her straps, adjusting first one, then the other. The warmth of his hands sank into her. Her nipples strained against the cups of her bra, the blush of her areolae just visible.

"My nipples do show." She tugged on the bra, but he stayed her hand.

Slowly, he turned her to face the mirror. "How does it make you feel?"

Heat surged through her as she stared at the exotic creature in the mirror. Who was this woman? She seemed even sexier than while wearing the merry widow, or could it just be Sam's undivided attention that added that extra glow?

"How do you feel?" he asked again, when she didn't answer. He stood behind her, pressed against her bare buttocks, his familiar scent surrounding her, the heat of his body warming her, calling to her.

"I feel..."

"Yes?"

"I feel...incredibly turned on."

"Yes." His hand left her hip and traveled up her side to cup her breast. "See how beautiful you are."

"Sam—"

"Sweetheart, do you know how much I want you?" His voice seemed pained.

She turned to him. The heat in his eyes held her transfixed. This singular display of emotion transformed him. Her pulse pounded. Her sex throbbed. She found herself fixated on his mouth. Had his lips always been that full?

"Tell me what you want me to do," she said.

An endless moment stretched between them, while her heart thudded in her ears. Finally, he spoke.

"Kiss me."

5

SAM'S GAZE LOCKED on Crystal's mouth. His request pushed the limit on her stipulation, but he stood, powerless to withdraw it. *Just this kiss.*

For one fleeting moment, he feared she might turn away. Then she was pressed tight against him, her arms wrapped about his neck and her lips full and inviting beneath his. She made a soft sound in her throat as she brushed his lips with hers, caressing them with an endearing hesitancy.

He started to pull away, but she followed, melting into him, her arms holding him in place. She opened to him, her tongue stealing into his mouth with a hunger that sent heat arrowing through him. Desire hit him in waves, rocked him with a force so intense, he vibrated with it. He deepened the kiss, running his hands down her back, then over the tight swells of her buttocks.

She felt so good.

A low moan escaped her. She threaded her fingers through his hair and cocked her hips, grinding herself against him. For long moments, he worshiped her mouth, reveling in every pass of her tongue, every whimper of desire he drew from her as he kneaded her firm flesh.

Guilt and common sense warred in him. Twice

more he attempted to withdraw, maintaining a thin hold on his control and cursing himself as the biggest fool to ever walk the planet. But each time she gripped him tighter, melding her body so closely to his, he wondered how he'd ever be able to stop.

At last she drew back, her face flushed, her lips swollen and her eyes heavy lidded and filled with want. His blood pounded through his veins, roared in his ears. Never had she looked more beautiful.

How many nights had he dreamed of her gazing at him that way? "Crystal, you take my breath away."

"Really?"

"Yes."

Her cheeks dimpled. "So, that was okay?"

"The kiss?"

She nodded and smoothed her palm down his chest. "It was sexy enough? It turned you on?"

He nodded, mutely. So this was what it felt like to spontaneously combust. "And you?"

"Me?" Liquid warmth shimmered in her eyes. "Most definitely."

She cocked her head, and her forehead furrowed in question. "Can I ask you something?"

"Sure."

"Why have you never settled down with any of the women you've dated?"

He pulled back a little, surprised at her change of subject. He stared deeply into her eyes and pushed the truth further from her probing gaze, tucked it away in its own little corner where he could brood over it another time.

"You know I take it light—keep it fun," he said.

"But is it easy for you...not getting emotionally involved—keeping it light?"

Sure it was easy. No woman he'd ever dated had compared to the one he'd always wanted. He'd never offered more than he could give and had never asked for anything in return. "Easy enough."

Until now.

"You see? You're the answer to all my prayers. You're already mentoring my makeover. We'll just have to broaden your job responsibilities...let you make me over in every possible way."

His pulse thudded in his ears. "How so?"

She straightened and looked him square in the eye. "You'll teach me how to *be* sexy, through hands-on, interactive encounters."

A buzzing sounded in his ears as he stared at her for one long, unbelieving moment. "You want me to teach you about sex, by having sex with you?"

"It just...feels right."

"You're doing it again."

"Doing what again?"

"That thing you do—running on impulse."

"And that's a problem, because...?"

"Because you're not stopping to think it through."

"You should try it sometime, Sam. Just let your emotions run free and see what happens."

He pulled her hands from around his neck. "That'll get you hurt, is what it'll do."

"No. I promise. I want to give it a whirl. None of the relationships I wanted in any serious way in the past ever lasted. And, yes, I did get hurt, on occasion.

"So, as a side benefit of your mentoring, I'll learn to be more like you. Keep it light." She stuck her nose in the air. "And you won't be able to harangue me with your gloom-and-doom predictions that Ron will break my heart. I'll keep it light. My heart won't ever be his to break."

Sam let out a frustrated groan. What would be worse: not encouraging her to shut off all her emotions, helping her to land Kincaid and fall madly in love with him, only to have her heart inevitably stomped on; or going along with her insane plan, knowing full well she'd be having mindless, emotionless sex with Kincaid?

"And your stipulation?"

Her gaze burned into his. "No holds barred."

He stared back at her. Did she know what she was saying? What she was agreeing to?

I'll...submit to you.

"Come on." She slipped her arms back around his neck and snuggled up against him. "We can keep all the emotional attachment out of it. I don't see why we can't remain friends through this. In fact, knowing each other and feeling as comfortable with each other as we do, should enhance the experience."

Her words hit him like a kick to his gut. Was this all he'd ever have of her? Emotionless sex. He lifted his chin and drew his pride up around him like a shield. "But what about our friendship? I value that, Crystal. You're not afraid we'll screw that up?"

Her eyebrows came down. Her eyes took on a serious light. "I do value our friendship. I promise I won't let this screw it up. You're very important to me, Sam."

"And you think you can do this and not get attached?"

She hesitated, her forehead creased, then she nodded with finality. "I can do it. Tell you what, if either one of us, for any reason, has a change of heart—like if I can't keep it light—then we'll call it quits."

A change of heart. Not likely. He was already in too deep to find his way out or he would have done so years ago. Of course, that wasn't what she meant.

Could he really take what she offered and come away unscathed?

She shrugged. "I'm not looking for love, if that's your concern."

No, he knew better. She'd never love him, not after he taught her how to wring all the emotion out of a relationship. And he definitely wasn't going to let himself fall for anyone else. He'd had enough heartache for one lifetime.

"So, you'll do it?"

"If I agree...what's in it for me?"

Her eyebrows arched. "Besides the obvious?"

"Besides the obvious. You're asking me to go out on a limb here, probably mess up our friendship. That's a big risk. I need a big payoff."

A mischievous gleam lit her eyes. "You can dress me up, if you want to."

"That's already part of the deal. What else?"

"Undress me, if you want to."

He let his gaze travel her length. "I wouldn't mind a little more of that."

She placed his hand on her breast. "Play with me...if you want to."

The last she issued as a challenge. He kneaded her breast, enjoying the sensation of her firm flesh beneath his palm, his desire building to an almost unbearable level. With his thumb, he teased her nipple through the silky fabric.

His groin tightened uncomfortably. He was damned anyway. He might as well take what little she offered. It would have to last him a lifetime.

He stuck out his hand. "Deal."

Her eyes turned dark and sultry as she placed her hand in his. She regarded him for a long moment, then asked, "So...what's next?"

Closing his eyes, he drew in a deep breath. He'd sold his soul to the devil and she was a blue-eyed, platinum-haired demon. He opened his eyes to meet her questioning gaze. "Get dressed."

Surprise arched her eyebrows. "But, aren't we going to...you know?"

"Oh, we're going to all right. Just not here, where we might be interrupted. This place is getting ready to close. And, honey, once we get started, we're not stopping until we've covered all the bases."

He picked up her clothes, then dressed her, yanking off the tags from her bra and panties. "I'll have them scan these, so you can wear them home."

"Sam," she said as he gathered up the assortment of lingerie.

"Yes?"

"Thank you."

He lifted her chin with the crook of his finger. "If you get what you really want from all of this, then you can thank me."

He turned her toward the door, visions of their night to come drifting through his mind. If this was all he was to have of her, he was going to make the most of it. He was going to make this one night neither one of them would ever forget or he'd die trying.

CRYSTAL BREATHED A SIGH of relief as Sam pulled into his garage some twenty minutes later. The ride to his house had been a blur of traffic lights, dodging other cars and the overwhelming sense that her life had taken on a surreal quality. At some point between when he'd stepped into that dressing room with her and when they'd left together, she'd discovered the true meaning of the words *turned on.*

Whether it was a sudden change in perspective, chemistry or some new sex virus, her body burned for his touch. He turned to her, then slid from the driver's seat, hauling her out of the car with him. He pulled her to his side, taking on most of her weight. She clung to him, breathing in his heady scent, skimming the salty taste of his ear with her tongue and relishing the feel of muscle beneath his shirt.

She'd always acknowledged that he held more than his fair share of sex appeal. How had she managed to remain unaffected until now? Had she suppressed some secret attraction all these years that had somehow sprung loose when he'd stepped into that dressing room?

The strong column of his neck drew her attention as he half carried her into the house. She traced her lips over his taut skin, from his chin to his collarbone. Then she darted her tongue in the hollow of his throat.

"Mmm, you do taste good," she murmured, before running her tongue along his jaw to his ear.

A low growl escaped him and he lifted her. "It's my turn to taste you."

In a few long strides, he dropped her unceremoniously on the bed, tumbling on top of her. His mouth claimed hers with no warning, stealing her breath and her reason with the insistent sweep of his tongue. His hands seemed to touch her everywhere and everywhere he touched seemed to come alive with new sensation.

"I want you naked." The roughness of his voice more than hinted that he was as aroused as she. He plucked the pins from her hair to let it cascade around her shoulders.

She smiled as his hands swept up her torso, taking her top with them. "Undress me, if you want to."

"Oh, honey, I want to."

He made short work of disrobing her, pausing to stroke his hand over the thong panties, before whisking them off her. In what had to be record time, his own clothes joined hers on the floor. She wondered at all her sexy new clothes and lingerie, still in bags in the car. She'd have to make a point to seduce him in each outfit, letting him peel each layer of clothing and lingerie from her heated skin.

Her breath grew shallow as she let her gaze travel over him. His body was magnificent. She'd seen him often enough, shirtless and in nothing much more than his boxers, but she'd never before quite appreciated the exquisite cut of muscle favoring him in all the right places.

Light from the night side table played off the smooth planes of his chest and washboard stomach. And his erection stood as an enticing monument to his desire.

Her own desire stirred to new heights. Had she ever

seen anything more beautiful? She reached out to touch him, but he clasped her hand to his chest.

"I'm calling the shots, remember?"

She nodded.

"This first time, I do all the touching."

"But—"

"No buts. Am I or am I not in charge?"

"Yes, but—"

"If you touch me, it'll all be over before it starts. And now…" Heat simmered in his eyes. "We play."

His body covered her and this time his mouth joined his hands in their exploration. His lips tickled and nibbled, while his tongue probed, excited, then soothed. He kissed her again, long and hard on her mouth, until she shifted beneath him, urging the length of his erection toward the aching juncture of her thighs.

"Not so fast." He rose up on his arms, his belly brushing hers. "First, tell me what you want."

"I want you."

His eyes closed briefly, then he dipped his head and kissed her breast. For long moments, he laved her with his tongue, working her nipple into a hard peak, while he strummed his fingers over its twin.

"Oh, Sam, I want you." Heat poured through her, pulsed in her sex, making her hot, making her wet, ready—past ready—for him to take her.

"Not yet. Tell me what you want me to do to you."

His gaze caught hers, as he moved to her other breast. Without breaking eye contact, he suckled her, teasing her nipple with his lips, tongue and teeth, while her nether lips grew slick with her desire.

"I want you to make love to me, to thrust yourself deep inside me again and again." She moaned and squirmed beneath him, trying to rub her throbbing clit along his erection.

He shifted his lower body away, while his mouth continued to work its agonizing magic on her breast. After a moment, he lifted his head to gaze at her with heavy-lidded eyes. "Are you so sure you want me to take you now?"

"Yes, yes."

"No, not yet. You're not quite ready."

A short laugh escaped her. "I'll burst into flames if I get any more ready."

"No, I'll say when you're ready. I want you to want me more than you've ever wanted any man."

"I do. I've never wanted anyone like this." To her horror, a note of desperation colored her admission, but damn it, it was true. The man was driving her stark, raving mad with the most delicious need.

As if he hadn't heard her, he resumed his ministrations to her breasts, toying with her taut peaks, until she moaned with every pull of his mouth. At last, he shifted and though he continued his tender assault, he slipped his hand between her legs to trace her swollen sex. He moaned softly, his tongue slowing its circling of her nipple, as his fingers explored her cleft.

"I want you...I want you." She gasped as he drew hard with his mouth and thrust two fingers deep inside her. She opened her legs wide for him, drawing her knees up to give him all the access he needed. "Ahh...yes, that's good."

He trailed kisses down her torso to her stomach, as he withdrew his fingers to circle her clit, spreading her wetness over the straining nub. She slid her hands over his chest, but he drew back, frowning.

"No touching, remember?"

A frustrated groan was her only response.

Clenching handfuls of the sheet to keep from touching him, she watched in growing anticipation as he moved down her body. He raised his head, his breath warm on her thighs. "Tell me what you want me to do to you."

"Kiss me...there."

"Here?" His gaze fell to her sex.

"Yes...please." She nearly cried in relief when his mouth closed over her.

He laved her, his tongue traveling over every fold and crevice, dipping into her slick entrance, before centering on her clit. Sounds of passion tore from her throat. When he took her into his mouth and sucked, she almost came up off the bed. Again, he slipped his fingers inside her, thrusting in a rhythmic beat.

Fire licked through her. For endless moments she rode wave after wave of pleasure as he loved her with his mouth and hands. She wanted to sob when he slowed, then stopped suddenly and rolled away from her.

"Sam?"

He didn't answer, but took a condom from a small box on his nightstand. She threw her arm over her eyes and drew a few long breaths, willing him to hurry. The bed shifted and his weight came down on top of her, his erection pressing against her.

She lowered her arm and met his intense gaze. A thrill ran through her, as he settled himself more firmly between her thighs. At last, she'd find release.

"Tell me what you want, Crystal. Say the words."

"I want you inside me. I want to come with you deep inside me."

Slowly, he pushed himself into her, stretching her, filling her, sending waves of exquisite pleasure rippling through her. She tilted her hips and ran her hands up his torso. "Now, can I touch you?"

Seeming at a loss for words, he nodded as he withdrew, then thrust again into her, beginning the ageless dance of lovemaking. Only this was like lovemaking she'd never experienced before.

Never had her senses been so acute, her responses so overwhelming. Had he drawn out their foreplay, denied them both this pleasure, while he kindled her desire to a near breaking point, knowing every cell of her being would respond to their joining?

Time collapsed, then suspended, as he loved her with his body, his scent blanketing her, his erection hard and hot inside her. Tension coiled through her. Cries of pleasure rose in her throat as he thrust again and again, bringing her to the brink of oblivion.

Then the world seemed to explode around them. She cried out and stiffened in his arms. Wave after wave of release rolled over her.

He thrust once more and moaned, his body gripped in orgasm. She welcomed his weight as he collapsed over her, hugging him close, cocooning him in the tangle of her limbs. For long moments they lay together, too spent to move.

Sam drew a deep breath and etched the moment into his mind: Crystal's earthy scent, her heart thrumming steadily beneath his ear, her body gloving him, while her tight passage contracted with tremors of her release and she held him as if she'd never let him go.

Warmth and contentment filled his chest.

But is it easy for you...not getting emotionally involved?

He pushed the thought away and rolled to his side, taking her with him. She was his. For now, she was his.

He brushed her hair from her cheek and smiled down into her drowsy eyes. "Don't go falling asleep on me now. We're just getting started."

Her lips curled into a smile. "Your wish is my command," she said, her voice like sunshine brushing over him. "Do I get to touch you more this time?"

"Do you want to?"

"You are...very touchable."

She trailed her fingers over his chest, tracing little circles around his nipples. "I like the feel of your skin. So smooth...and you have all these muscles. They just ripple when you move. You're so sexy, Sam. I just never thought you would ever want me like this. I'm not anything like the women you date."

"No, you're not. You're unique. One of a kind."

Her mouth rounded into a thoughtful pout. "Is that a good thing?"

"Oh, yeah." He dipped his chin and kissed away her pout, delving again into the rich depths of her mouth.

Her tongue met his, her stroke playful and sure. She smoothed her hand along his shoulder, his back, down his spine to his buttocks. Her fingers traced over him, circling toward his hips, then over his thigh.

"Hold on just a sec." He slipped from her arms to

pad across the floor to the bathroom. He cleaned himself, then returned, a glass of water in hand.

After drinking deeply, she set down the glass and he pulled her to him. He kneaded her breast, then kissed his way down her neck to the soft curves, taking her nipple into his mouth and savoring the feel of the beaded peak against his tongue.

Moaning softly, she slipped her hand over his groin to his cock. With a deft touch, she stroked him to arousal, her fingers playing first softly, then more insistently over him.

"Do you like that?" she asked, her face a mask of concentration as she focused on pleasuring him.

"Sweetie, I'd like pretty much anything you did right now, as long as you're touching me. And as long as you're actually enjoying yourself."

Her expression lightened. "I am enjoying this. I just want to know everything about pleasuring you. Are certain ways I touch you better?"

"Like this." He placed his hand over hers and guided her fingers around him, then drew her hand along his length.

The pink tip of her tongue flicked out as she concentrated. Fire seared through his veins. He shifted. "Let me touch you, too."

He nudged her knees apart and slipped his hand between her legs to that part of her that waited wet and swollen for him. Her eyes widened and the little sigh of pleasure that escaped her as he slid his fingers over her pulsing sex nearly undid him.

He matched the rhythm of her strokes, thrusting two fingers deep inside her, until her eyes glazed and her breath came in little pants. Her fingers slowed, then stilled, as she lost herself to the sensations he stirred in her.

A flush covered her cheeks and chest as she rocked against him. Mewling sounds of pleasure flowed from her lips, as her gaze locked on his. With one final thrust of his fingers, she came again, her liquid heat spilling over him, her eyes wide with wonder.

He closed his own eyes and held her. How would he ever survive past this night? Surely he'd die of sheer pleasure before they were through.

When her breathing settled, she stretched in his arms like an overindulged cat. Then her eyes narrowed, as she slid her hand along his erection. "Now, where was I when you distracted me?"

"Ah." He breathed the word out as she pulled on him. "Right about there."

"I want to kiss you here."

Desire spun through him. She lowered herself over him, her warm breath skimming his heated flesh. He bit back a moan, as she glided the pointed tip of her tongue from the base of his erection to the tip.

"Hold me...here." He guided her hands to his balls. She cupped him first tentatively, then more boldly. Her tongue flicked over him, tracing the rim, then darting across the bulging head.

For long, torturous moments she laved and kissed him, then, when he thought he might not be able to bear any more, she took him into her mouth.

The sweet pull of her lips brought his hips off the bed. He moaned her name and threaded his fingers through her hair, entangling them in the silky mass. His body shuddered, nearly out of control as she kneaded him, while loving him with her mouth.

He gritted his teeth. ''Crystal, you have to stop.''

She shook her head, the motion drawing another moan from him. His body tensed. How would she react should he lose the thin grip he held on his control?

''Sweetie, you'll make me come if you don't stop.''

At last, she slid sensuously up over him, rubbing the length of her body over his. He could only stare at her, speechless. She was a goddess and why she'd gifted him with this night was beyond him.

''I'm sorry,'' she said, the sultry tone of her voice sending ripples of warmth along his spine. ''I've never done that before. I didn't realize how…how powerful it would make me feel…how incredibly turned on.''

''Crystal…'' He traced her cheek, awed by her beauty, by her giving nature.

She closed her eyes and moaned softly. ''I feel like I'm on fire.''

''I think I can help.''

He rolled her to her back, fighting the temptation to take her again. He wanted to draw out their loving—make it last the whole night. He kneeled beside her. ''Show me where it burns and I'll kiss it and make it better.''

Her teeth closed over her bottom lip. A sigh of anticipation escaped her, as she parted her thighs. Drawing her knees up, she tilted her pelvis toward him, fully exposing her swollen sex, her clit, straining for his touch.

Breathing deeply of her desire, he took her with his mouth. He thrust his tongue into her quivering passage, then kissed her all over, before moving to her clit. With firm motions he licked circles around the straining bud. She shuddered and moaned beneath him, her hips moving in a steady rhythm. She strained and ground against him as he traded his attentions between the hard nub and her slick passage.

"Sam…Sam…oh, Sam." Cries of pleasure tore from her as he flicked his tongue over her. He teased her, nipping and sucking and laving her, until she tossed back her head and cried his name again.

The orgasm ripped through her and still he held her fast, drinking deeply of her liquid heat, kissing her softly, until the tremors passed and she lay limply, her eyes closed, a becoming flush covering her entire body.

He leaned back and absorbed the picture of her lying there, sated, her every charm spread before him, like a feast he'd long craved, but had never been able to partake of. He breathed in her scent and let his gaze drift over each detail: her peaceful expression, her nipples rosy and peaked and her sex swollen and wet with his loving.

As if she sensed his intent perusal, she opened her eyes and gazed shyly up at him, drawing one knee down in a half-hearted attempt at modesty. "You are a god, Sam. I'm not sure how you've done it, but you seem to have unleashed something in me. Something insatiable."

"Touch yourself." The command left his lips before he'd fully formed it in his mind.

Her eyes widened and her lips parted, then she ran her hand down over her breast, along her belly, to touch herself where his mouth had been.

His breath caught and his cock stirred when she dipped her fingers into her cleft. "Show me what you like, sweetheart. How you want to be touched. How you like to pleasure yourself."

"I've never done this in front of anyone before."

"Show me. I want to watch you."

He locked his gaze with hers for a long moment before focusing on the arousing sight of her fingers disappearing into her passage. He swallowed and guided her other hand to her breast. "Touch yourself here, too. You know what you like—what feels good."

His erection throbbed as she quickly brought herself again to the brink of orgasm. Her body writhed, straining toward release as her fingers worked their magic over her own flesh. Again, her cries of pleasure floated over them and he couldn't hold back a moan of his own. He burned for her.

With a final thrust, she came, her body frozen in orgasm. He grabbed a condom from the nightstand, whipped it on, then rolled her to her belly, whispering in her ear, "Draw your knees up. I'm going to take you again."

Eyes closed, she nodded.

He settled between her thighs. As he lifted her hips, her round bottom brushed his erection nearly undoing him. She moaned softly and moved her knees under her, as he entered her from behind. Her passage was tight and rippling with aftershocks of her climax.

Any control he'd maintained up to that point fled, when her heat surrounded him, gloving him, gripping him with a force that took his breath and shook him to his core. For mindless moments he thrust into her, lost in a haze of lust and passion. Tension coiled through him as ripples of indescribable pleasure teased him, taunting him with fulfillment. Again and again he thrust, taking her with an almost savage exuberance.

Only she existed. Crystal.

His Crystal.

She twisted around to him, her eyes like liquid fire, her mouth open in a soundless moan. She rocked back into him, meeting him thrust for thrust, her movements as frenzied as his. Then she came again, her orgasm gripping them both with an intensity that rocketed him over the edge.

His own release left him limp, his heart pounding.

He clutched her close to him, their bodies still joined. As he breathed deeply to calm his pounding heart, one thought played through his mind: He loved her and he'd love no other for the rest of his days.

It was a damn shame.

6

CRYSTAL AWOKE TO A SOFT breeze on her face and Sam's solid form at her back. She lay for a moment, soaking in contentment. Her body warmed at the memory of his tongue stroking hers, his fingers strumming her nipples and his erection hot and pulsing inside her.

She'd slept with Sam.

A shiver of arousal rippled through her. Before yesterday, she never would have thought to do such a thing. Since then, it seemed she didn't want to do anything else. Even now, she wanted him again.

The notion of Sam as her sexual mentor had hit her with such clarity in the dressing room. It had seemed inevitable—the answer to a multitude of questions. How had she not thought of it sooner?

Last night had eclipsed all her previous sexual experiences, as limited as they were. This morning she felt altered, as though he'd lifted her out of her everyday world and dropped her into a real-life fantasy, where she cast off her image as one of the guys and stepped into the role she was meant to fill—that of seductress.

"Mmm, somebody's sleeping in my bed." Sam's gruff voice pulled her from her thoughts as his arm tightened around her and scooped her back against him.

The image of herself as seductress fled and her heart quickened. Feeling inordinately shy in the light of day, in spite of the night they'd shared, she rolled to her side to face him. "I'm awake."

"Did you sleep okay?" His heavy-lidded gaze lingered over her bare breasts, before settling on her face.

She nodded and pulled the sheet up to her neck, silently chiding herself for her silliness. The man had already seen every inch of her. Hadn't she lain open-legged and sated before him?

After they'd finally finished making love in the wee morning hours, she'd lain awake with the wonder of it. All this time, she'd been chasing some fulfilling, emotional, possibly unattainable relationship. She'd been missing out on all the fun.

At long last, she had drifted off to sleep, then slept like a rock. Now she ached in places she hadn't known existed. "Did you?"

"Sleep well? Like the dead."

He brushed a stray lock of hair from her cheek. His eyes took on a warm glow. Did he realize he was letting his guard slip—showing his inner feelings? How different he seemed—how enticing it made him.

Who knew such warmth and vibrancy lurked beneath his usual stalwart exterior?

His fingers traced along her jaw. "You look thoroughly mussed."

"Oh..." She smoothed her hand over her tangled hair, embarrassment pricking her. "I'm horrible at morning-afters. You wouldn't happen to have any good pointers?''

The warmth fled from his eyes. ''We don't have to constantly be having lessons, Crystal. It's okay to relax and enjoy yourself around me. You don't have to always be 'on.' I wasn't criticizing you. I happen to like you looking like you've had a good night of loving. It's very sexy.''

''I'm sorry.'' She blew out a breath and tried to smile, but something like panic seemed to take hold of her.

Her heart sped and a slight ringing sounded in her ears. What did he mean about not having a lesson and relaxing around him? Did he want to have sex with her outside the realm of their arrangement?

''You don't have to apologize.'' He nuzzled her ear. ''A little good-morning kiss might be nice, though.''

His mouth closed over hers before she could answer. As his tongue teased past her lips, sexual excitement curled through her. Still, even as she kissed him back, her mind filled with doubt.

What if they weren't able to go back to being friends? What if he didn't want anything to do with her once he'd transformed her and helped her win Ron? The possibility of losing his friendship suddenly had her paralyzed.

Why *hadn't* she thought this through?

He pulled back, concern drawing down his eyebrows. ''What's wrong?''

She swallowed and tried to push aside her worries. Sam cared about her. He wouldn't desert her. Besides, they'd already taken the plunge. There was no going back now.

This was the price she'd pay for her impulsiveness.

"I just...I don't know what to say or do. I mean, after last night..."

After last night, what? She was having all these confusing feelings about him? Like she enjoyed waking up to his warmth beside her, his arm heavy across her waist? She loved the way he made her feel as if she was the most special woman to ever walk the earth? She wanted to see more of that enticing light in his eyes? She wanted desperately to know if he now felt anything other than friendship for her?

Regret stole over her. He was suddenly all too exciting and her plan to cash in on his expertise to help her gain Ron's interest had somehow lost some of its appeal. Funny how she hadn't thought of Ron until now.

Sam regarded her a long moment, his face its usual mask. "Last night was...last night."

Thrilling, exhilarating, possibly life-altering. Her heart thudded. Had he felt it, too? In light of this incredible new adventure they'd embarked on, would he ask her to drop her cause to win Ron?

"You want to know about morning-afters?"

She nodded, her gaze never leaving his.

"This is prime keep-it-light time."

"Oh." Her hopes faded.

"We need a plan." He scooted into a sitting position.

"A plan?" She straightened. For their new future?

"Right. Now that we've got you all dolled up

and...*educated* on the fine art of seduction. I think you're ready for a test run.''

She sat up beside him. ''What kind of test run?''

''One where Ron gets an eyeful of the new you.''

''Oh.'' A wave of disappointment washed over her, but she did her best to stifle it. Wasn't this what they'd agreed to? She'd promised not to get her emotions involved.

What had she been thinking?

She shifted, mentally shaking herself. She had to get a grip. She had to keep it light. ''You're right. We need a strategy.''

She slipped from the bed, tugged Sam's T-shirt over her head, then paced across the thick carpet, breathing in his scent from the shirt and doing her best to ignore the pounding of her heart. If Sam was going to stick to their no-strings arrangement, then so was she. She was a missile, honed in on her mission to catch Ron's eye. It was still a good plan. Ron was a great catch—all she'd ever wanted in a man.

Sam eyed her lazily from the bed, the sheet low on his hips. ''Honey, all the strategy you need is to have him see the new you. He'll be all over you then.''

She paused in her pacing, letting her gaze sweep over him, before snapping her eyes forward. She couldn't let her newfound attraction to Sam confuse the issue or distract her in any way from her goal. Sam had made it very clear he wasn't looking for love.

''Well, okay, but how will he see me? We need to plan the details of this sighting. It has to look casual, unplanned, of course, but we should orchestrate it, as much as possible.''

"All right."

"I was thinking we could manage an accidental run-in at that restaurant he likes."

"Nava—that southwestern place. That'll work."

"Do you know when he eats there? Does he have a certain day of the week he goes?"

"If I'm not mistaken, he'll be there Wednesday night. With a date, of course."

"Of course." Her stomach tightened. "Of course he'll have a date. But so will I."

"You will?"

"Well, yes, *you*, silly."

"I see. Make him jealous."

"Maybe, I'm not sure...but if you act as though you're really interested in me, it might somehow make me seem more desirable."

Sam shook his head. "I don't know why you're worrying about this. I'm telling you, you wear that black number we bought yesterday and that'll be all you need. The man won't notice I'm there."

"He'll probably be with one of those models. We can't take any chances."

"I'd be happy to charm his date from him, if it will help your cause."

She stopped in front of him, the thought of him turning on his charm for Ron's date further twisting her gut. "Well, I wouldn't want you to lead her on or anything."

A short laugh burst from him. "No ma'am. I shoot straight from the hip. Nothing on my agenda but the obvious."

"Right." She frowned, her earlier doubt assailing her. Keeping it light wasn't as easy as she'd hoped.

"What is it, sweetheart?" He patted the bed beside him.

She paused for only a moment before slipping under the sheet next to him. "I know it's a little late to be asking this, but…I just want to make sure. Are we still friends? Last night didn't change that, did it?"

She drew a deep breath and held it. He captured her gaze for a long moment before answering, his expression revealing nothing of what he was thinking. At long last he spoke. "I'm whatever you want me to be. Nothing will change that. I promise. Our friendship will remain unaltered as long as you want it that way."

A mixture of relief and chagrin flooded her. They'd made a deal, this was a no-strings affair. She squelched the confusion of emotions clamoring through her, and forced a smile. If he could stick to their agreement, then so could she.

"Thank you, Sam. I wasn't sure if the sex would confuse things. Mess them up for us."

He scooped her into his arms, rolling her to her back and pinning her beneath him. "Did you enjoy last night?"

Warmth flooded her cheeks as his heat pressed down on her and memories from the previous night flooded her. "You couldn't tell? I honestly have never been so multiorgasmic before. I had no idea I could just keep coming like that."

"Do you feel like it helped you, then?"

"Oh, yes. You make me feel…so desirable. Not at all like one of the guys." She cocked her hips, pressing her pelvis against him, the warmth in her belly expanding outward. "I never knew I could be so...uninhibited in bed."

"Then it was well worth it. Just good sex between friends. What harm was done?"

Just good sex between friends. His words were meant to comfort her, but they left her feeling a little hollow. "None, I suppose."

"Right." He tugged the sheet down to her hips, then stroked his hand along her side, over her waist. "So, you'd like a morning-after lesson?"

She sighed as he cupped her breast and thumbed her nipple. She was on safer ground in her role as pupil. Willing pupil. "It's Monday. Don't you have to get to the office?"

"They'll manage without me for a bit. I'm sure everyone will appreciate my relaxed mood. Can your deadline wait a little longer?"

How could she even think of writing, when her body begged for more of his loving? "Maybe just a little longer."

"First, as far as morning-afters go, it's best to keep the focus on the physical. You can talk about all you enjoyed with each other's bodies, but feelings are a taboo. Sensations are another thing, though. Let's get rid of this. Your body is beautiful. When we're alone like this, I prefer you naked." He stripped his shirt from her, then lowered his head, closing his mouth over her nipple.

She moaned softly as he suckled her. "So, you like having sex in the morning?"

A low chuckle escaped him. "Sex in the morning can be even better than sex at night."

"Better than last night?"

"Last night was just the warm-up."

"Oh." Excitement raced up her spine.

"Let's try that kiss again."

He brushed his lips over hers and she opened to him, welcoming the insistent thrust of his tongue and the feel of his body pressed close to hers.

He took his time kissing her, his tongue dueling with hers, one hand sliding down to cup her bottom, while the other toyed with her nipple. As before, his touch aroused her, so she soon moaned into his mouth and undulated against him.

When he at last ended the kiss, she bit back a cry of protest. He patted the pillow beside him. "Lie back and get comfortable."

She settled as he asked, her heart thumping in anticipation. She let her gaze sweep over the broad expanse of his shoulders, his solid chest. How could she ever have looked at him and not felt this liquid heat stirring in her?

"Now, I'm going to play with you and I want you to tell me everything you're feeling. Tell mc what you like and how you like it."

"Okay, I'll try. Do I get to touch you this time?"

"All you want."

She skimmed her hands over his chest, toying with his nipples as he'd done to her. A shiver of excitement rippled through her when he closed his eyes and moaned, his erection pressing into her belly.

"I love this." She slipped her hands down to stroke his hardness from straining base to bulging tip. "I like touching you. I really liked…kissing you all over last night. I never wanted to do that before, but you made me so hot and I just loved the feel of you against my tongue—in my mouth."

He shuddered, moaning softly. He kissed her thoroughly again, while she continued to stroke him. His hands cupped her bottom, kneading her, pressing her against him.

His mouth left hers to trail kisses down her neck, over her chest to nuzzle her breast. Then he shifted his lower body away from her tender explorations, as his tongue flicked over her nipple and she sighed.

"Tell me. Tell me what you like," he urged.

"That's nice. I like when you kiss me there. I get so hot when you play with my breasts."

His teeth scraped over her sensitive flesh, before he took her into his mouth and suckled her again, while rolling her other nipple between his thumb and forefinger. Heat shot to her core and again she moaned. "That gets me so turned on, Sam."

He raised his head as he slid one hand down between her legs. "Are you wet for me?"

"Yes."

Her breath escaped on another sigh as his fingers strummed over her. "Oh, yes, touch me there. That feels so good."

"Open for me, Crystal. I want to see you—all of you."

She raised first one knee, then the next, following his lead as he guided her legs out of his way. She lay before him, open and exposed and pulsing with need.

Then his mouth was on her. His tongue teased her clit as his fingers delved deep inside her, escalating the sexual tension, until she writhed beneath him.

"Oh, Sam, yes, kiss me there. It feels so good. That's it...there...oh, yes, right there."

He continued to lave her clit with hard fast strokes. Liquid fire seared her veins. She gasped for breath and moaned, unable to speak, letting the sensations take her. He quickened his pace, thrusting his fingers in a faster beat, as cries of pleasure tore from her throat.

"Do you want me, Crystal? Do you want me inside you now?"

"Yes...yes."

"Touch yourself, while I get ready for you."

She needed little encouragement, as he rolled away to slip into a condom. Closing her eyes, she circled the finger of one hand over her clit, while kneading her breast with her other hand, her nipple taut against her palm. Sexual tension built to a nearly intolerable level.

"Hurry, Sam, I need you."

His gaze remained fast on her, as he rolled on the rubber. She nearly cried out in relief when he grabbed her by the hips and then rolled to his back, bringing her on top of him. "Ride me."

With a tilt of his hips, his erection pressed into her. A low moan escaped her as he filled her, stretched her. She moved over him, experimenting first with a roll of her hips. "So...good."

"Like this." He guided her with his hands, coaxing her into a steady rhythm that had them both holding on and groaning with ecstasy.

Pinpoints of fire spun all around them. Crystal gripped Sam's shoulders and rode him as wave after wave of pure sexual pleasure washed over her.

"Come with me," he urged.

She nodded, unable to speak as the first ripples of orgasm hit her. Her gaze locked on his and her release slammed through her with a terrifying intensity. His face seized in an expression of bliss so pure it tightened her throat and brought tears to her eyes.

She collapsed on top of him, burying her face in the crook of his neck, while he stroked her hair and murmured tender words into her ear. She couldn't make out what he said over the pounding of her heart, but her chest swelled and, for just that one moment, she let herself bask in whatever emotion seemed to be enveloping them.

Sam's own heart beat a steady tattoo beneath her ear. A feeling of feminine pride swept over her, empowering her as never before. With his help, she'd attained a level of sexual prowess she'd never even contemplated before. And it was all due to his somehow freeing all her inhibitions.

She felt strong and powerful and sexy. A satisfied sigh escaped her. Convincing him to teach her the art of seduction had been the smartest thing she'd ever done.

IT WAS THE DUMBEST THING he'd ever done.

That Wednesday evening waiting for Crystal to get ready, Sam squeezed his eyes shut and tried in vain to blot out the memory of her riding him as he'd never been ridden before, her eyes round with excitement, her cheeks flushed, her breasts swaying in sync with the hungry thrusts of his body. As it had done thousands of times since, his groin tightened into what he feared might be a permanent state of arousal.

Thoughts of their night—and their morning-after—had plagued him. Sometimes the memories hit him so hard he'd close his eyes and will his heart to cease pounding, while he filled his mind with budget figures and ad deadlines. He'd passed the hours hiding out in his office, his emotions running rampant between anger at the thought of her with Ron and excitement over the inevitability that he'd soon be with her again.

She'd ruined him for other women. Every woman—administrative assistant, executive or model—he'd encountered on his rare ventures from his hiding place had failed to measure up to Crystal's standards. It was a mystery how he'd managed to focus on the magazine at all.

What had he been thinking? How was he ever to talk to her, to look at her, the way he had in the past? Sure, he'd fantasized what it would be like to be with her—to make mad, passionate love to her—but the reality had far surpassed his every expectation. Her cries of passion still rang through his memories. He'd never get the feel or taste of her out of his mind.

And he had to. She still wanted Kincaid.

A small part of him had hoped that once he and Crystal had actually had sex that she'd forget about the guy. That she'd realize he, Sam, had been the one she'd wanted all along, but she'd started that morning eager for another lesson—eager to be that much closer to her goal of transforming herself.

For Kincaid.

Well, she'd managed to transform herself, all right. Sam leaned back against the headboard and braced himself as she emerged from the bathroom. When he'd finished struggling with the current issue at the end of the workday, he'd made a quick stop at his place to shower and change, then headed back to her place.

She'd been primping and grooming herself for over an hour now, reciting Loni's instructions as she went. She'd gotten her makeup and hair just right, though he'd been thrilled to find her freshly scrubbed from her shower on his arrival. The telltale cutoffs and T-shirt on the bathroom floor revealed she'd slipped back into the old Crystal during the day.

But as she stood before her closet, clad in only a towel, searching her new wardrobe, she was every inch the seductress once again.

Tonight, they'd "accidentally" run into Kincaid at Nava, his favorite restaurant. Sam shook his head. The man didn't stand a chance. One look at the new Crystal and Kincaid would be smitten. Sam's job would be done.

A wave of regret flowed over him. Knowing she'd abandoned her plan for a meaningful relationship and was now dedicated to keeping it light—having purely sexual relationships—didn't make matters any easier to handle. Somehow, just when he'd had a taste of what it would be like to have her for his own, he had to find a way to let her go.

If only he'd had a real shot with her.

He gritted his teeth as Crystal glanced back at him, her forehead furrowed in question.

"The black one." He rose, then crossed the carpet to where she stood before the full-length mirror, holding several dresses in front of her.

"It isn't too much like what every other woman

will be wearing—like what his date will probably be wearing? You don't like the red?"

"The red is great, but you should save it for a special occasion. For tonight, wear the black." He lifted the other dresses from her, then hung them back in the closet. "And underneath..."

He brought her a demibra and matching thong panties they'd picked up on their way to the register during Sunday's shopping spree. With deft movements, he loosened her towel, so it fell in a soft pool around her feet. Kneeling before her, he slipped the panties up her legs, settling them around her hips. Then he stood and hooked the bra around her. He took a moment to adjust the straps, relishing the soft curve of her breasts as they rose and fell with her breath.

He stood behind her, drinking in her clean scent. "Do you like it when I dress you?"

She turned in his embrace and looped her arms around his neck. "I like it when you touch me. Even when you're just dressing me and not making love to me, it turns me on. You can be gentle...or not and I seem to like it all." She took his hand and kissed his palm. "You have a magic touch, Sam."

He closed his eyes and tried to pretend that he readied her for an evening alone with him—not her debut at seducing Kincaid.

"Does it matter what I wear underneath? Who would know if I wore my cotton panties?"

"I would know...and you would know."

"Right." She looked at him expectantly.

He smiled. How could the same woman, who'd been totally uninhibited in bed, still be so naive? "How do your cotton panties make you feel?"

She shrugged. "Cool, comfortable."

"And how does this—" he swept his hands down to cup her bare buttocks "make you feel?"

"Not cool and comfortable."

"You're wet, aren't you? This lingerie turns you on."

"Exactly, which works great for when it's just the two of us, here—alone. But I'm afraid I'll feel exposed and not at all confident in public. Is it necessary?"

"Like you said, only you and I will know what treasures lie hidden under your clothes. All everyone else will see is the flush on your cheeks and the fire in your eyes."

He lifted her chin. "One look and Ron will be yours. How could he not envision you in his calendar, after seeing you in this dress?"

She lifted the dress, rubbing the silky fabric between her fingers. "Do you really think so?"

"No man will be able to resist you tonight."

"I'm...not sure. Maybe we should arrange something more private."

"The restaurant is a good plan. It will seem more spontaneous this way. Unless...you want to stay in with me tonight. I'd be happy to further your education."

She gazed at him for one long, heartrending minute and he hated the hope that rose in him. He was ten times a fool to want to continue the torture of pretending she was his. At last she dipped her head and stepped into the dress.

"You won't leave my side?" she asked.

"Never." He helped her thread her arms through

the straps that held the dress in place, zipped up the back, then smoothed the garment over her, reveling in the feel of her firm body beneath his hands.

"So, you'll be my date tonight—at least for appearances' sake."

He nodded grimly.

"Should we pretend we're a couple? I mean it wouldn't hurt to have Ron think you find me desirable. I do want him to know I'm available, though."

"We'll play it by ear. I'll follow your lead. It wouldn't be difficult for me to appear like I'm totally smitten with you."

She laughed. "Right, Sam. That'll be believable."

"Why wouldn't it be?"

"Because you never appear smitten, or anything else for that matter."

"Yes, I do."

"Never. Not as long as I've known you. You hardly ever so much as crack a smile, even when you're kidding around. You're the Iron Man."

He stared at her in disbelief.

"It's true. Don't look at me like that. The one and only time you've ever shown what you were feeling was..." Her voice trailed off and pink tinged her cheeks.

"Was when?"

"Nothing. Just act like you always do. Anything else will look suspicious. Ron'll know it's not real."

He gazed at her as she ran her brush one last time through her hair. He'd told her to leave it down tonight. It was the way he would want her to wear it, if this were a real date.

She slipped on a pair of her new strappy sandals

with the three-inch heels and turned to him. "Ready? We'd better go before I lose my nerve."

He was all for her losing her nerve, but a deal was a deal and he meant to see her through this trial. The sooner he handed her over to Kincaid, the quicker Sam could cut his losses and run away to lick his substantial wounds.

As he followed her out, he let his gaze travel over the enticing curve of her buttocks. It seemed his fantasies alone had gotten him through the past few days. He might as well make the most of the night.

In the eyes of the public, this evening she'd be his. He meant to make the most of it. He reached her side and let his hand roam possessively over the curves he'd just admired. She pressed herself to his side and gave him that coveted smile of hers.

Taking a deep breath, he squelched the urge to throw her over his shoulder then head back into the house. Instead, he held the car door for her while she slipped into the passenger's seat, her floral scent teasing him when she brushed by him. Tonight, she was bound to capture the photographer's attention, as well as any man's in sight. Perhaps tomorrow Sam would have his new columnist and the magazine would be on its way to winning a National Magazine Award.

He should be thrilled, but the sick feeling in his gut told him an award-winning magazine, let alone any controlling interest, would do little to warm his bed.

7

CRYSTAL STOPPED INSIDE the restaurant's threshold and breathed deeply of the mingled scents of nameless delicacies that made her mouth water and her stomach growl in a most unladylike manner. Sam turned from the black-garbed host and offered her his arm. They followed the host past other diners in the dimly lit, adobe-walled room. Woven pillows lined the back of a bench along one side of a row of tables and various metal sculptures dotted the walls.

"There he is," he said, his tone grim, as he nodded to a table to their left.

A wave of nerves hit her as she followed his gaze to where Ron sat at a table with a stunning brunette. The woman looked every inch the calendar model. Crystal glanced down at her own black-clad figure. The outfit had seemed sexy when Sam had helped her into it and the approving gleam in his eyes certainly meant he'd been impressed, but as she wobbled across the marble floor she felt like an imposter.

What had she been thinking?

Her heart raced when they passed within a few tables of the couple. Shrouded in self-doubt, Crystal kept her eyes anchored to the seating host's back, willing him to place them well away from Ron and his date.

''Schaffer!'' Ron's familiar voice rose above the restaurant's hubbub. To Crystal's distress, Sam fell back and raised his hand in greeting as Ron motioned him over.

Sam threw her a sideways grin and cocked his head in Ron's direction. ''Just as we planned.''

''Hold on.'' She glanced at their seating host, who stood waiting patiently.

Sam leaned around her to the man. ''Excuse us. We'll be right back.''

He took Crystal's elbow and steered her through the maze of tables. Seeming to sense her nervousness, he gave her arm a comforting squeeze. ''Relax, sweetheart. You're a knockout. Not a woman in here comes close.''

She nodded mutely and forced her feet toward the table. Ron rose and pumped Sam's hand. ''Hey there, bro. Got a taste for the good life tonight?''

''Always up for spoiling myself and my lady, of course.'' Sam turned meaningfully toward Crystal.

Ron's smile brightened, as his gaze drifted over her. ''You *are* moving up in the world, Schaffer.'' He extended his hand to Crystal. ''I don't believe we've met. Ron Kincaid.''

Heat burned her cheeks as she took his hand. ''Crystal Peterson.''

His forehead furrowed. He cocked his head in question.

''She scored the winning touchdown Saturday,'' Sam supplied, a note of disdain in his voice.

Ron's eyes widened and he gripped her hand a little tighter. ''Peterson?''

She nodded.

"My God...Crystal...look at you. I didn't even recognize you."

She shifted her weight, not sure if the emotion rolling through her was triumph or embarrassment. She had wanted him to notice her and it seemed he had, but somehow his newfound interest felt a little too close to insulting. Had she been so unattractive before?

She pulled her fingers from his too-tight grip and glanced at the woman at the table.

"This is Sheila." Ron waved his hand at the woman, his gaze fast on Crystal.

"Sheila." Crystal extended her hand. "I'm Crystal."

"Right." Sheila gave her a cursory shake from her chair. "The football player."

Something in the woman's tone had Crystal stiffening. Sam dropped his arm around her shoulders and pulled her to his side. "She gives us all a run for the money."

He introduced himself to Sheila, who beamed him a bright smile. The woman's predatory gaze had Crystal bristling. An unprecedented wave of possessiveness swept over her. She glanced back toward their seating host, who spoke quietly with one of the wait staff.

"We should go," she said.

"No. We won't hear of it, right, Sheila?" Ron pulled out a chair beside him. "You must join us."

Crystal's unease intensified. "We couldn't intrude."

"Sure you could." Sheila grabbed Sam's arm and tugged him toward a chair. "We insist."

"Well...if you insist." Sam waved on the seating host, then glanced meaningfully at Crystal.

Her heart sped. Wasn't this what she'd wanted? "All right...if you're sure."

She slid into the seat Ron held for her. Sam settled in the open place opposite her, between Ron and Sheila. The woman immediately shifted toward him, her ample cleavage angled for his view. "Perfect timing. We were just seated ourselves. I thought I was in the mood for something light." Her gaze swept to Ron, then back to Sam. "But I'm suddenly craving something with a little more gusto."

The sultry tone of her voice had Crystal stiffening in her chair. Was the woman openly hitting on Sam? Crystal glanced at Ron to gauge his reaction.

To her surprise, he let loose a hearty laugh. "Watch out, Schaffer, I think you've been targeted. Guess the lowly photographer's been thrown over for the big-time publisher. I should warn you, she's as finicky as a cat."

Sheila gave him a disapproving look. "Don't be silly. I wouldn't make a play for the man in front of his date. I'd at least wait until she'd gone to the ladies' room."

They all laughed lightly over her comment, while Crystal stifled the urge to strangle her. What nerve. Sheila had no idea that Crystal was after Ron. For all she knew, Sam could be her one and only.

"Crystal, you are stunning tonight." Ron shifted closer, letting his gaze again drift over her. "Why have you been hiding yourself all this time? I had no idea."

Again, that confusion of excitement and disappointment swirled through her. Sam's snort of derision caught her attention. "She's been there all along, Kincaid."

Ron shook his head, apparently ignoring Sam. "So, what do you do...when you're not scoring touchdowns?"

The waiter stopped by to take their order and Crystal heaved a sigh of relief. Ron made her nervous enough without her having to explain that she spent her time writing fluff for the nation's women's magazines. Besides, he was just making polite conversation. What interest could he possibly have in how she spent her days?

He turned to her as their apron-clad waiter retreated. "You are absolutely stunning. Tell me, have you ever done any modeling?"

A nervous laugh escaped her. Her plan was working almost better than she'd hoped. Why then did she feel a little nauseous? "No, not really."

"I tried to talk her into competing for Miss Milton High our senior year." Sam shifted forward, his gaze encouraging Crystal. "The closest she got was riding on the back of the senior-class float in the homecoming parade."

"You went to Milton?" Ron regarded her with new interest. He shook his head. "Were you hiding yourself then, too?"

"Well, I didn't dress like this, if that's what you mean," Crystal answered.

"For what it's worth, I heartily approve of the new you. What brought on the transformation?"

Crystal blinked at him. *I have the hots for you, so I made a deal with my friend, Sam, here, to make me over and teach me about seduction, in a very first-hand way, so I can try my wiles on you.*

"She's researching a makeover article she's writing for *Woman's Day.*" Sam gave her a reassuring wink.

Relief flowed through her. Leave it to Sam to cover for her.

"So, you're a writer?" Ron leaned closer. The spicy scent of his cologne wafted over her.

"Yes, I freelance."

Sheila settled back in her seat, her arms folded across her chest. "So, you're doing a makeover article?"

"Actually, it's a series of articles, right, Crystal?" Sam nodded reassuringly toward her.

"That's right."

"How sweet." Sheila clasped her hands in an obvious fabrication of delight. "What else do you write about? The secret lives of housewives? Nail care dos and don'ts? Hairstyling tips? That would make fascinating reading." Sarcasm rang clearly in her voice.

"Actually, Crystal's articles have drawn much acclaim. She's won several awards. Tell them, honey."

She didn't know whether to bless Sam or bash him over the head. He was trying so hard to be helpful, but somehow accenting the fact that she excelled at fluff didn't seem quite the right route to take. "Just a few industry awards, nothing too exciting."

Ron nodded, his gaze intent. "So, do you like freelancing—living from project to project? Something new and different always waiting for you."

She nodded as a sense of dissatisfaction filled her. He made it sound so exciting, when she thought of her work as a means to keep a roof over her head and food in her stomach. Yet, at one point, hadn't she felt that excitement, too?

"That's fascinating. I'm a freelance photographer. Maybe we could collaborate on a project sometime."

"I'd like that."

This was the perfect opportunity to ask him about his current projects. She opened her mouth, but a fit of nerves prevented her from saying anything, so she smiled awkwardly, then took a gulp of wine.

Their food arrived and the conversation lulled. Crystal bit into her filet mignon, calculating the cost of each bite in her weekly budget and chiding herself for missing the opportunity to broach the subject of his calendar. How could she now tactfully bring it up?

I hear you're shooting a lingerie calendar and I'd like to be one of your calendar hotties.

"So, Ron, I hear you're shooting a new calendar." Sam threw her a quick wink, as he peppered his food with gusto. "How's that going?"

"It's starting to shape up. We've decided on a locale for the shoot, a quiet, beachy spot in the Florida Panhandle. The client is an older couple who own several lingerie shops in town. They're hoping the calendar will help them build name recognition and product awareness. Now it's just a matter of finding the right models to help make Secret Temptations lingerie more memorable."

"They have this wild line of erotic wear," Sheila added, her eyes wide. "I just love going into their shops. I actually met Norma and Charles Craig, the owners, there the last time I was in."

Crystal straightened. ''Yes, I know that shop. We were there this weekend. Weren't we, Sam?''

He nodded, his green gaze fixed on hers. ''Yes, we had quite a pleasant afternoon acquainting ourselves with the merchandise.''

''Oh...'' Ron straightened. ''I thought you were just good friends, but *are* you two actually dating?''

He gestured between Crystal and Sam. All eyes turned expectantly to Crystal, Sam's included. Heat bloomed in her cheeks. What exactly were she and Sam?

She laughed lightly, hoping no one noticed the little catch in her voice. ''Sam is advising me on a new wardrobe. I'm doing that makeover series and decided to make myself over, so I consulted with an expert. With his background at *Cosmo* and his work on *Edge,* who else would be a better advisor? Plus he knows me better than anyone...''

Open for me, Crystal. I want to see you—all of you.

The memory of Sam kissing her intimately Monday morning swept over her. He held her with a steady gaze, no hint of his reaction to her words evident in any way, yet guilt assailed her.

She looked away, forcing herself to take a bite of her steak. They'd said no strings, no attachments. Somehow, she felt as though revealing what they'd shared would bring it into an emotional light—make it real.

It couldn't be real. Sam didn't want that. And neither did she. She wanted Ron. She threw him a sideways glance, smiling as she choked down her food.

Like a golden god, he regarded her, a curious light in his eyes. ''So, you're not dating anyone?''

She kept her gaze on him, but Sam's eyes seemed to burn into her from across the table. "No...there isn't anyone."

"Hard to believe," Ron said.

Sheila scooted her seat closer to Sam. "So, does that mean you're up for grabs?"

"Actually, I *am* seeing someone." Again, his gaze held Crystal transfixed.

Her heart gave a little flutter. Was he talking about her? Then another thought flitted across her mind, bringing a new sense of unease.

Was there someone else?

Sheila pouted most prettily. "Well, I would share."

Sam patted her hand and smiled indulgently. "I'll keep that in mind."

Her well-plucked eyebrows arched in disbelief, then she turned to Ron with a laugh. "Sugar, looks like you get lucky tonight, after all."

Those dimples that drove Crystal to distraction broke out on Ron's cheeks. He grinned across the table at Sheila. "I live to serve."

Crystal tossed back another big swallow of wine. This night wasn't quite heading where she'd hoped. Ron was supposed to be eating out of her hand right now, not making plans to bed his date.

"You serve it up and I'll eat it anyway you want." Sheila took a bite of her creamy seafood, then licked her lips in a suggestive manner.

Ron made a growling sound in his throat, but if Crystal wasn't mistaken, his half-lidded eyes depicted more boredom than sexual interest. Hope rose in her. Maybe she was right. There was more to him than Sam gave him credit for.

Which meant she still had a chance.

She may not be ready to jump in the sack with him, but her instincts told her if she waited until after they'd become better acquainted to sleep with him, they'd both find something, if not meaningful, then at least of equal enjoyment. But how was she supposed to get to know him when he always seemed to have someone like Sheila around to distract him?

"THAT WENT WELL." Sam palmed the wheel as they took a wide left turn.

A feeling of satisfaction filled him. Surely the evening had been an eye-opening experience for Crystal. After facing the stark reality of Kincaid's shallow attitude toward women, surely she would feel inclined to give up her plan for a purely physical relationship with him. Maybe now she'd drop her pursuit altogether.

Crystal stared at him in disbelief. "And how do you define well? Because as far as I can tell, he just went home to have wild sex with Sheila."

"Right, but he'll be fantasizing that it's you."

"Great, that's just what I wanted."

"He noticed you."

"But he went home with her."

"She was his date."

She shrugged and peered out the window. "I wanted to make a really good impression on him—knock his socks off. If I'd actually done that, he wouldn't be off playing whoopee with another woman—date or not."

"Playing whoopee?"

"You know what I mean."

"That's unrealistic. Sheila's a sure thing. It's got nothing to do with you. No guy in his right mind would pass that up."

"You did."

He came to a stop at a light and turned to face her. "I must not have been in my right mind, then."

"Why did you? Pass her up, I mean."

She had absolutely no appeal compared to you. "She's not my type."

"Sure she is. She's long-legged with all the right curves, just like all the other women you've dated. And she certainly seemed inclined toward purely physical relationships. You two would have gotten right along there."

The light changed. He gunned it through the intersection. "Maybe I've decided I want more than a pretty face."

"And a knockout body."

"And a knockout body."

"Really? You would date an average-looking, overweight woman?"

"Maybe, if we had chemistry and she had some depth to her."

"Depth?"

"Yes, depth."

"This from the man who likes to keep it light, who believes relationships are meant for fun."

"I've had a change of perspective lately."

"Since Sunday?"

"Maybe watching you doll yourself up to be eye candy for Kincaid has gotten me thinking. Maybe I don't think a woman should have to go through that kind of transformation for any man. Maybe we should all start appreciating women from the inside out."

"This is not just about being eye candy for Ron. The exterior is just to get him to notice me. Once I've achieved that, then we'll have a period of time where we date and get to know each other. Then, when we're both ready, we'll take it to the next level."

"Wild sex, like he's having tonight with Sheila."

"You've taught me to like wild sex."

"Well, at least you're not talking fairy tales anymore."

"For your information, Mr. Cynic, just because I'm now redefining my relationships, does not mean I no longer believe in meaningful interactions. Men and women enjoy that kind of thing all the time."

"So practicing cynical behavior does not make you a cynic?"

"Not at all. I may be trying something new, but I still have hope that, one day, I may stumble on a meaningful relationship. I just don't see the point in looking for one. I'd rather enjoy myself along the way."

"Well, you won't stumble on it with a guy like Kincaid. I'd be willing to bet he just doesn't have it in him."

"Not that it matters, but that's not fair. You say you've changed. Well, maybe he'll change, too."

"For your sake, if that's what you ultimately want, I hope so."

"I told you. I'm not looking for that from him. First, I would like to establish some kind of rapport, though. So what did you mean?"

"About what?"

"About seeing someone. You told Sheila you were seeing someone."

"Oh."

"What did you mean? Are you seeing someone?"

"I'm seeing you, sort of."

"Sort of."

"We have this…arrangement."

"You're mentoring me."

"Correct."

"And that's what you meant."

"Yes."

"So, you used me and our 'sort of' relationship as an excuse not to have sex with Sheila."

"I didn't need an excuse not to have sex with her. I just could have said no thanks."

"But you didn't."

"No. Why are you making a big deal out of this?"

She sat back in her seat, staring straight ahead, as they entered the ramp onto 400. "No big deal. The truth is real—it has depth. Isn't that your new thing? Why didn't you just go with that?"

He gripped the wheel and refrained from looking at her. Frustration simmered in his gut. How could he even think about being with another woman? No one else would ever satisfy him the way she did.

"That *was* the truth. I *am* currently seeing you."

"Even though our relationship, with its purely physical nature, lacks this new depth you're looking for."

"I like to finish what I start. In fact, I'm considering giving up women for a while, when we're through."

"You're joking."

"Nope."

"But why? I don't believe you. That's the most ludicrous thing I've ever heard you say."

He risked a glance. "Maybe I've decided I want more than good times in a relationship."

"You want depth." Her eyebrows arched in disbelief.

"And why is that so hard to believe? Look at Steels—what he and Paige have. Maybe I'm starting to want that, too."

"Wow…I'm…I'm stunned. But even if you actually do this, which, frankly, I can't believe, I don't see how giving up women is going to accomplish that. Doesn't a woman—the right woman—figure into that scenario?"

"I'll just quit dating until I find her."

"You mean, except for me. We still have our 'sort of' relationship."

"Except for you. But while I'm mentoring you, I don't want to be with anyone else, in case it taints the process."

"Taints the process? What does that mean?"

"It means, I like to focus on one project at a time. It's just the way I work."

"So, I'm a project."

"That's right. I give you the education you need to hook up with Kincaid. You write my column."

"I make an *effort* to write your column."

"That's all you'll need."

He took her hand and squeezed it. "I have a good feeling about this. All you need to do is put forth the effort. The rest will fall into place. I know you have your doubts, but you'll see. Your column will put us over the top. In fact, I'm counting on it to land us one of those National Magazine Awards next year."

"Sam."

When she didn't continue, he glanced over at her. Her eyes were rounded as she stared back at him. He gave his attention back to the road. "What?"

"The National Magazine Awards? You're putting all *that* on me?"

She'd probably flip if he told her about the controlling interest. "Your column will clinch it for us next year. I can feel it in my bones."

"Don't do this to me."

"What?" He glanced at her again. This time deep grooves furrowed her forehead and her folded arms plumped up her lovely breasts.

"I don't work well under pressure."

He laughed. How could she know so little about herself? "Yes, you do. You never lose your concentration, you always keep your head and you tend to finish first. Look how you scored that touchdown Saturday. That was par for you. It would have been so easy to choke, but you didn't. You came out of it smelling like a rose. Just like always."

A strangled sound that may have been an attempted laugh escaped her. "You're talking about sports."

"So? It's all the same. Pressure is pressure."

"No, it definitely is not. One is physical, which anyone can handle if they've trained enough and the other is purely intellectual."

"And your point is?"

"I don't handle that kind of pressure well."

"Crystal, it's all a matter of attitude. You believe in yourself when we're out on that field. You believe you can catch that ball and run like hell when we need you to. You believe in your ability to score.

"Well, this is the same thing. I'm counting on you to carry us to the awards. You've got the talent. You've got the brainpower. I believe in you. All you need is to believe in yourself."

"It's not that simple."

"Yes, it is, if you would just relax and allow it to be. You're the one who's supposed to be so good at letting it go. Just let it happen." He turned to her. "Look, our deal was for you to give it your best effort."

"But you have these enormously high expectations. You're putting unfair pressure on me. I can already feel myself choking."

"If you choke, you choke. We'll all get over it. No big deal. But you have never choked a day in your life. You can't blame me for having a little confidence."

"Great. This is just great."

"Tell you what, why don't you think up a few article ideas and we'll toss them around tomorrow night. I'll stop by after work."

He pulled into an empty spot in front of her apartment and cut the engine. The streetlight that normally lit up her small corner of the lot had apparently gone out. Darkness pressed in around them and the nocturnal sounds of the lake permeated the air.

"I can't get to it until after I'm through this deadline."

"Okay. When will that be?"

"Maybe by the middle of next week, or by the weekend." She shrugged. "I may be able to fit it in between deadlines. I'm really booked through the end of the month. I have to start the makeover series next."

"Fine."

"So, do you want to come up?"

He drew a deep breath, torn, knowing each night of ecstasy with her would make it that much harder to give her up. "You think you still need more mentoring?"

"What did I do wrong tonight?"

"Honestly?"

"Yes, honestly. I felt like I was making progress there in the beginning, but then it was like Sheila completely stole the show. If I can't compete with someone like her during a mere dinner, how will I ever make it into that calendar?"

"Body language."

"Body language?"

"Right." He adjusted his wheel up, so he'd have more space, then turned to face her. "Here, let's pretend you want to seduce me."

"I'm not sure I'm ready to seduce him. For now, I just want to get to know him better. Just because I want to keep it light, doesn't mean I want to rush into anything."

"Well, the only way you're going to manage that with Kincaid is to have an attitude of seduction."

"You're sure?"

"Think about the calendar. Every man who looks at it is going to fantasize that every woman in it is wanting him. That's the attitude you'll need to get across in that shoot. But before you get to the shoot, Ron has to see that attitude for himself."

"Okay, so how do I pull off this attitude of seduction? I use body language, right?"

"Yes, but you have to also have the mental part down. That's ninety percent of it."

She blew out a breath and leaned toward him, her features just recognizable in the darkness. "So, I think sexy thoughts, right?"

"Right."

"Like with you, I can think about how I feel when you touch me." She blinked and wet her lips.

His gaze riveted to her mouth and the heat started low in his belly. "Think about the things we did last night that excited you."

"Like when you kiss me and caress my breasts."

"Right."

His gaze dropped to her breasts and it was all he could do not to touch her. "Think about the sensations of my mouth on you. You really like when I kiss you there, don't you?"

"Yes. I like when you play with my nipples and touch me between my legs."

"See how you're leaning toward me? How open your body language is? And your eyes..." He became lost for a moment in the heat of her eyes.

He did reach for her then, slipping his hand behind her neck and bringing her closer. "Your eyes are saying you want me to kiss you."

"Yes," she whispered as she leaned into him.

Her mouth joined his in a hungry rush of lips and tongues. She slipped her hands up his chest, caressing him through his shirt. He moaned softly and lifted her onto his lap, then slid his hands up under her dress. He loved the feel of her bare ass in his hands.

8

THE CURSOR BLINKED the next afternoon, mesmerizing Crystal. She stared at it another moment, her mind swirling with a fog of thoughts, none defined or clear enough to record.

"Damn." She pushed away from her desk and rubbed her hands over her face.

Her deadline for this latest article loomed, but since she'd started all this makeover business, she'd hardly written a word. Each time she sat before her keyboard willing herself to focus on the trials and tribulations of family reunions, thoughts of Ron and, more insistently, thoughts of Sam intruded until one seemed to cloud over the other and she sat in a state of confusion that grew worse with each passing day.

She stalked into the kitchen to pour herself a fresh cup of coffee, grimacing at the one she'd left sitting on the counter to grow cold over an hour ago. She grimaced again as she caught sight of her reflection in the toaster. What would either man think of her now?

She'd put on one of her flirty new dresses in an effort to stay in character, but her hair hung from a ragged ponytail, and, though the toaster made a poor substitute for a mirror, it did appear as though she was growing a major zit on her chin.

Some calendar model she made.

She'd shower and transform back into her new self in a little while. Sam was sure to drop by again after work and he'd no doubt give her hell for backsliding. Her spirits lifted. She still had a number of new outfits with which to seduce him. Not that she spent much time in her clothes once he arrived, but that was half the fun. And the heated look in his eyes when he saw her was enough reward for her efforts.

After adding liberal amounts of sugar and creamer into her coffee, she stirred it slowly, then took a tentative sip. The oversweetened taste had her frowning, and she scowled at the sugar bowl, but then took another swallow anyway.

"Okay, family reunions. I can do this." She glanced at her calendar.

Five days. She had five days to finish this piece and get it off to her editor at *Redbook.* How difficult could that be? It wasn't as if she were writing a novel. And she was halfway through the thing.

"Okay, no more distractions." She carried her coffee back to the desk, then plopped herself in her chair.

Ten minutes later, she stared at the blinking cursor, a sinking feeling in the pit of her stomach. She couldn't do this. What had ever made her think she could make a living from writing?

The ringing of her doorbell startled her. With a mixture of irritation and relief, she headed for the door. She opened it to find her mother on the step.

Sarah Peterson beamed at her daughter, her honey-colored hair pinned in a neat French twist. "Hello, sunshine. What a pretty dress. What have you done to yourself? You look different."

"It's nothing, Mom. I've overhauled my wardrobe. Come in."

Her mother stepped inside, but hovered in the entryway. "I'm not staying. I know you're probably in the middle of a writing streak. I'm off to buy new furniture for the house now that we've decided on a color scheme. I have carpet and drapery swatches in the car."

"That's nice, but don't you think you should wait until after you close?"

"Nonsense." She waved a hand in dismissal. "I've been waiting twenty-five years for this house. I am not going to waste a moment in enjoying it."

"Now—" she looped her arm through her daughter's "—I was thinking maybe you'd have a minute to come with me. I just loved that article you did last year on decorating faux pas and I'd love to have an expert along."

"I'm not an expert. I've written a few articles. Here, I'll get you copies to take with you. Then you'll have the total of my expertise at your fingertips."

Her mother's eyebrows drew together. "No, sweetie, if you don't have the time, I'll go alone. I just thought it would be fun. We could catch up, have some lunch. I haven't seen you in a while."

Crystal shrugged, trying to dispel the irritation grating through her. Why her mother's obsession with this house aggravated her, she couldn't say, but if she had to spend the afternoon focused on choosing plaid over paisley for that mausoleum of theirs, she'd scream.

Besides, she had this deadline.

"Sorry, Mom, I have to get this article done. Can I take a rain check?"

Disappointment shadowed Sarah's expression, but she straightened and attempted a smile. "Of course. I should have called."

"No problem. I'll give you a shout when I have some time. Maybe next week."

The light ignited again in her mother's blue eyes, eyes a shade or two darker than her own. "Sure, sweetie, you can help me pick out the bathroom accessories. We've got four full baths in this house. I want to do a nautical theme."

"Sounds great." Crystal hugged her mother close, then said goodbye, relief flowing over her as she closed the door behind her.

"SO, HOW WAS NEW YORK?" Crystal dropped the bag of groceries on the table that evening, then flipped on the kitchen light.

In the hopes a trip to the store would help clear her head and exert her nervous energy, she'd showered, then made a quick run out for munchies. On her return, she had been surprised to pull into her complex behind her sister. It seemed it was family day at her apartment.

Megs shrugged. "People everywhere, traffic backed up. We took the subway. It had this funky smell. The apartment was small, but very luxurious. I could definitely get used to all the great restaurants and the shopping, though. Leo completely spoiled me. He was loving and attentive. He bought me anything I so much as looked at. I swear, I ended up with a whole new wardrobe. Not that I can fit into anything, after all the eating out we did. But, enough about me. You must have had some kind of week yourself.''

''Me?'' Crystal gazed at her sister in surprise. How could she know?

''Yeah, you. Sam did his thing with you, didn't he?''

''Excuse me?''

A smile curved her sister's lips and lifted her eyebrows. ''I don't think I've ever seen you so prettied up and just to run to the grocery store. He did your makeover.''

''Right, actually he did. This is the new sexy me.''

''I can tell, but I'm guessing somcthing else has got you preoccupied for you not to have noticed.''

''Noticed what?''

Megs stared at her a long moment, an unreadable expression on her face. Then she leaned forward and wriggled the fingers of her left hand under Crystal's nose. Light played off a huge diamond on her ring finger.

''Oh, my God!'' Crystal grabbed her hand and stared in awe at the ring.

''We were shopping one minute. The next thing I knew I was wearing this big rock. I'm still not quite sure how it happened.''

''What do you mean? Didn't you say yes? Didn't you tell Leo you'd marry him?''

''Not exactly.''

Crystal gazed, wide-eyed, at her sister, waiting for her to continue.

''I just...he asked if I'd given it serious thought. I said yes, meaning I'd really thought it through. He thought I was saying *yes* yes and he was so happy I couldn't bring myself to correct him."

"So, did you mean to say no?"

"I don't know. I wanted him to give me some more time, but we haven't set a date and I'm sure by the time we do, I'll have made up my mind."

"But, Megs, that's insane. You have to tell him. You shouldn't lead him on."

Grooves formed between Megs's eyebrows. "I know, but I just can't right now. He's already called his parents and the rest of his family and friends. I think he sent out a mass e-mail. His mother called me last night about the rehearsal dinner and she contacted a cousin of hers, who's a florist. She's arranged for him to do all the flowers at a discount. Leo's family is all over this."

"You do *not* have to go through with this. You need to tell him you need a little time. If he loves you, he should understand."

"He does love me."

"Then you know what you need to do, hon."

Megs just stared at her, her eyes round and forlorn.

"Wouldn't it be better to break it to him now, rather than wait until you're both standing at the altar with all of his family and friends present?"

"I know. I know. It's just that I really don't want to hurt him and there's a very good chance I'll want to go through with this whole thing and marry him."

"A very good chance is still not definite. He has a right to know that you have concerns—that you're not absolutely sure, yet."

"So, what did you do this week?"

"Why are you back to that? You are not going to

avoid the issue, my dear. I certainly didn't go get myself accidentally engaged. My week did not consist of anything quite so drastic.'' Her cheeks warmed.

Sleeping with Sam *had* been pretty drastic.

''But you did do something—something that was out of the ordinary.''

''Now, what makes you think that? Just because I didn't notice your ring doesn't mean I did anything unusual this week.''

''I'll make you a deal. You tell me what you did and I'll talk to Leo.''

Crystal stared at her sister, openmouthed. ''You can't blackmail me into telling you anything, especially when there's nothing to tell.''

''Methinks you protest too much.''

''Fine. Don't say anything to Leo. Let this whole wedding thing snowball. Why would you follow my advice?''

''Why are you worrying about me? Maybe it's time I started being a little spontaneous. Besides, I thought you said I never made mistakes.''

''That was before you got yourself engaged without intending to.''

''I think you're making a big deal out of my situation because you don't want to deal with whatever you did this week.''

''That is a load of crap.'' Crystal grabbed her purse, then stormed out of the room.

She needed to do something—anything—just to get out of the house. A feeling of rebellion rose up inside her. She should celebrate her transformation. That's what she'd do. Small and tasteful. Yes, that was it.

She'd get a tattoo.

...CONSIDERING THE ACTIVITIES planned, allow extra time in dealing with the inevitable friction that comes from bringing together—

The ringing of her doorbell stopped Crystal in mid-sentence, breaking her train of thought. Damn, just when she'd finally started writing again. She hit Save. While the computer whirred softly, she rose to see who could be stopping by in the middle of a Friday afternoon, grimacing at the slight pain in her ankle where the permanent likeness of a small butterfly now resided.

She yanked open her door, fully expecting to find neatly dressed door-to-door salespeople on her front step. Instead, a stunning woman who could have stepped out of any one of Sam's magazines stood smiling at her.

"Yes, may I help you?" Crystal narrowed her eyes on the woman, who, on closer inspection, seemed shockingly familiar. "Cami?"

Cami smiled a red-lipped smile and tossed her sleek hair. Not a trace of bed head remained. "It's the new me. What do you think?"

"I think I need to sit down."

Feeling as if the world had turned topsy-turvy, Crystal headed for the comfort of her sofa. She plopped herself unceremoniously onto the overstuffed cushions. A sense of discontent settled squarely over her.

Sam swearing off women, Megs acting impulsive, now Cami looking like an *Edge* model. Was her life ever going to be the same?

"You don't like the new me?" Cami followed her in, then twirled on her spike-heeled sandals, the hem on her short skirt billowing in a little cloud around her.

"You look great—better than great. You just don't look like you."

"Of course I look like me. This is the new, improved me." She waved her hand. "You'll get used to it."

"What was wrong with the old you?"

Cami plopped down beside her. "Nothing. She's still here. What are you all sour about? I mean, *you're* one to talk." She eyed Crystal's crop top and short-shorts. She made no comment about the tattoo, but her eyebrows archcd.

"I am *not* sour. I'm working. I have an article due—a deadline, remember?"

Her aggravated tone seemed not to faze her friend. "Oh, are you working on that makeover piece?"

"No, not yet. I have to finish this how-to on family reunions, first."

"How's it going?"

"There are some real horror stories out there, but I'm showing how this one family successfully incorporated the old with the new."

"What did they do?"

"You know how when you go home, everyone still thinks you're eighteen-years-old?"

Cami nodded.

"Well, this family has retained some of the traditions they used from when they were all growing up together—they meet at the same beach house they rented for family vacations of old—but they add a new tradition each year.

"For instance, the oldest son now runs a catering

business, so he throws a big cookout and they all get to see him in his 'new' role. They each take a turn planning an activity around one of their areas of expertise or current interests. It helps everyone see how the other family members have moved forward in their lives."

"That's cool. I like that—the merging of the old with the new."

"I think part of the problem with family reunions is that people tend to get stuck in all their old issues. This idea of bringing in updated traditions seems to help them develop new perspectives so they can move forward.

"But enough of that. Why are you here? Aren't you supposed to be at work?"

Cami waved her hands, so the bracelets on her wrists clinked. "I had a dentist appointment and we finished up sooner than I'd thought. There's no sense rushing back now, just to get caught in traffic. Especially since the office isn't expecting me."

She cocked her head. "So, maybe you can use this concept of merging the old and new in your makeover series. It's perfect—leave what's good, then redo the rest."

Crystal folded her arms and stared at this stranger, who happened to be her best friend. When had Cami ever given her advice on her articles? Not that there was anything wrong with her suggestion.

It would be easy enough to work in the theme.

"When you get ready to do the series, you can write about me. I'll do an interview if you want," Cami said. "I even have before-and-after pictures."

"'Right, I'll put you under 'Making Yourself Over to Pacify Your Lover.'"

Indignation widened her friend's eyes. "I most certainly did not make myself over to pacify Parker."

"Then why have you painted and primped and... rearranged yourself?"

"I guess for the same reason you did." She smiled at Crystal's aggravated expression. "I can't believe you didn't tell me. Besides the fact that your nails are painted and you're wearing mascara and that come-and-get-me-boys outfit, did you think you could show up at Nava, all spruced up and dressed to kill, and word not get out?"

Crystal shrugged. "Atlanta's a huge place. I would have mentioned it. Besides, what makes you think I went through a makeover for the same reasons you did?"

"Well, how many reasons can there be? I was tired of being one of the guys. Plain and simple, I was ready to express my feminine side."

Crystal sank back into the cushions. Why was she so mad at Cami? "Okay, maybe I wanted to do that. I wanted everyone—or at least Ron—to know I'm all woman."

"Oh, I hear you did that all right. You had all the men drooling."

"And where did you hear that?"

"Parker is really good friends with the chef, so he's treated like a VIP and we get takeout sometimes, even though they don't offer it as a regular service. We had our own little private dinner."

"So he likes the new you?"

She bobbed her head in affirmation. "He bought

me the naughtiest outfit from that new lingerie shop at Northpoint Mall."

"Secret Temptations?"

"Yes. You know it?"

"Been there myself." She shrugged. "We were there Sunday, in fact."

"Megs went, too? I thought she told me Leo was taking her to New York."

"No, I didn't go with Megs. I went with someone else."

"Really? Who?"

With a sigh, Crystal leaned forward, her gaze intent. "Sam took me."

"Sam?" Cami's eyes rounded.

"I asked him to help make me over."

"I can see that. He's got the background, that whole *Cosmo/Edge* thing, but—"

"But wasn't it weird lingerie shopping with my good male friend?"

"Wasn't it?"

"It was...surprising."

Cami leaned forward, her eyes alight with curiosity. "Really?"

"He got—we both got...turned on."

"Oh, my God, you and Sam?"

Crystal bit her lip and nodded.

"Oh...my...God."

"My sentiments exactly."

"In the shop?"

"We sort of got started in the dressing room, but we ended up back at his place."

Cami stared, openmouthed and grinning broadly.

"He called a little while ago. He's coming by after work to help me get ready for tonight."

"What's tonight? A romantic dinner—just the two of you? A midnight skinny-dip?"

"We're stopping by some gallery. A friend of Ron's is having a showing of her work. A female friend. Ron called Sam today and asked him to stop by...with me."

"Oh." Cami slumped back, a disappointed frown drawing down her eyebrows. "That's nice—cultural. I just thought with Sam, well..."

"Well what?"

"I just thought— He just has this—I don't know—earthy, even carnal, quality about him. If not for Parker, I would have gone for Sam long ago. I always imagined he'd be the type to dive into a sexual relationship. You know, forget about everything for a while and just bask in the physical side of things."

"*You* were interested in Sam?"

"Like he'd ever notice me, with you around."

"What does that mean?"

"Don't act like you never noticed the way he looks at you." A deep sigh escaped her as a dreamy look came into her eyes. "I always thought it'd be so romantic when the two of you hooked up."

"You're kidding. He never looked at me any way. I've definitely always been one of the guys where Sam's been concerned. Until this past Sunday, at least."

"If you say so."

"Of course I say so. Besides, there's nothing like that going on. There's no romance. We made a pact."

"Pact? What kind of pact?"

"No strings. No emotional attachment. He's just teaching me."

"What?"

"Well, it made sense at the time. I needed a more thorough makeover. I needed to know how to properly seduce a man like Ron and, well, it isn't like I've ever been all that good in bed."

"And he agreed to this?"

"Very willingly. Sam doesn't do complicated. At least he didn't used to, but I'm not even getting into that. This works for both of us. It's just sex."

"And that works for you?"

She shrugged. "Sure. And I think it may be helping. Ron seemed semi-interested at Nava."

Cami blinked. "You've already got one of the hottest guys in Atlanta and you're still after Ron?"

"I don't have Sam and what's wrong with Ron?"

"Nothing's wrong with Ron, but Sam—"

"Isn't interested in me for anything serious. Not that I'm looking for a serious relationship with Ron."

"How can you be so sure? That Sam's not interested, I mean."

"He was the one to bring up Ron after we…you know."

"Really?" Doubt weighed Cami's tone.

"Yes, really. We're lying there spent and I'm thinking, 'Wow, that was pretty incredible.' And I'm having these feelings."

"Yeah?"

"And he says, 'We need a plan.' And I say, 'Plan?' I thought maybe he was talking about a plan for us, but no, he starts talking about Nava and Ron." The words tumbled from her and Crystal blinked back confused tears.

"Oh, honey, so you have feelings for Sam?"

"I don't know. He's so good about this nonemotional involvement. I just have a little trouble with this intense physical closeness, then keeping it all light. But I did promise." She straightened and drew a deep breath. "Besides, I'm still infatuated with Ron, and I made progress with him the other night. He did at least notice me."

"And you're sure *he's* the one you want?"

Crystal took a deep breath and faced her friend. A confusion of thoughts whirled through her. But, ultimately, Sam had been very clear about their relationship. And her evening with Ron, though it hadn't quite ended the way she'd hoped, had certainly shown promise.

"Yes," she said with conviction. "Ron is still the man for me."

CLASSICAL MUSIC FILLED the air of the brightly lit, VIP-packed gallery. Atlanta's finest preened about, mingling and admiring the life-size photographs gracing the otherwise stark walls. The photos depicted people from all walks of life and cultures from around the world.

Sam set down his untouched glass of champagne and let his gaze drift, for the hundredth time that evening, over Crystal. A familiar warmth radiated low in his belly. She'd rolled her hair, then put it up in a loose twist. Her strapless dress whispered over her curves and hollows, teasing him with her every movement. Light danced in her eyes as she sipped her champagne and gazed at the crowd and the art that had brought them all together.

She caught him staring and ducked her head, smiling shyly in that way that made him want to scoop her in his arms and run away with her to some quiet, remote spot. "Sam, you have to quit looking at me like that."

"What's wrong with the way I'm looking at you?"

"You make me feel like the main course at a banquet."

"You do look most delicious tonight, even though your tattoo still looks a little sore."

Pink tinged her cheeks in a most becoming way. "I know I'm supposed to have you directing me these days, but I just couldn't help myself."

"It probably isn't something I would have thought of, but it works. I like it. It's all you, babe. You know, your impulsive nature is kind of sexy to me."

She smiled.

"You're radiant," he said.

"Stop."

"Ah, I sense it's time for another lesson."

She set down her glass, then faced him, arms folded. "Okay, if you think it will help. Ron's been so covered up with people since we got here, I don't think he's even noticed me."

"We'll combine two lessons, then."

"And they are?"

"First, we need to teach you how to flirt."

"Flirt?"

"Yes, the ability to banter conversation in a suggestive manner that has the object of your flirtation panting after your every word."

"Sounds complicated and like a lot of work."

"By the end of this evening, you'll be an expert."

"Promise?"

"If not, then you can take me home and ravage me."

"You're naughty."

"But nice."

"Yes. So, what's the second lesson?"

"How to make a man jealous."

"Now that sounds interesting."

"And lots of fun for me, since by the end of the evening, Kincaid will believe you want me bad."

"So, I use you to make him jealous."

"Yes. I guarantee that if you shower me with attention, cast me adoring glances at every opportunity and, of course, hang all over me, touching mc as much as is publicly permissible—lots of PDAs—he'll be panting after you in no time."

"You're sure?"

"He's always wanted what I have."

"And what do Palm Pilots have to do with it?"

"Not that kind of PDA. Public displays of affection."

"I see."

"Your basic hugging, stroking…and we should most definitely throw in a good dose of kissing."

"I don't know. Every time we kiss, we tend to end up…you know."

"Playing whoopee?"

The pink in her cheeks deepened. "Exactly."

He stepped closer to her. "Well, we could draw out the tension for as long as possible, work up a good craving, then either make a run for it or find a discreet storage room somewhere.''

''You're intolerable.'' She stifled a laugh.

He held up a warning hand. ''The first rule of flirting is that you shower me with compliments.''

''So, I can't say you're intolerable?''

''Only if your tone relays that you mean it in the best of ways.''

She repeated the sentiment, adding a breathless quality to her voice.

''Much better. See, that says you really like the storage-room idea.''

''Oh, Ron's looking.'' She smiled and waved.

''Not so enthusiastically.''

Her hand fell to her side. ''Maybe you should put your arm around me.''

''Okay.'' He slipped his arm around her waist and pulled her firmly to his side, savoring the softness of her curves and the warmth of her body. ''But the jealousy thing will work better if he thinks you're coming on to me, as opposed to me coming on to you.''

''Oh. So, I should do something like...'' She reached up and curled a lock of his hair around her finger.

''That's a start.''

''But?''

''But you need more.''

''Like this?'' She trailed her hand along his jaw, tilting his face toward hers. ''Then maybe this...''

Standing on tiptoe, she brushed her lips over his in a quick kiss.

When she would have drawn away, he slid his hand

to the back of her head and held her in place. She made one futile attempt to push away, then pressed in closer and kissed him back, laving his tongue with hers until he finally broke away himself, breathing hard and wishing fervently for that storage closet.

"Look, I think it worked." Her own voice sounded breathless near his ear. "Here he comes."

To Sam's annoyance, the man brushed by a curvy brunette vying for his attention and made a beeline for Crystal. Kincaid was way too predictable.

"Crystal." He took her by the hand and assessed her from head to toe. "You are looking fine tonight, love."

"Thank you." She glanced at Sam, then back at Ron. Her voice again took on that breathy quality. "And you're doing a fine job of...um, matching up your clothes."

Ron laughed and Sam shook his head as her eyes widened in bewilderment. They'd have to arm her with an arsenal of fail-safe compliments. Sam extended his hand to Ron. "Kincaid, nice party."

"Good to see you, Schaffer. What's up?"

"Just enjoying the ambience." He turned to Crystal who nestled into his side and gazed up at him adoringly.

Too bad it wasn't for real.

"I see." Kincaid's gaze again swept over her and Sam tightened his hold.

An elderly woman dressed in a peacock-blue gown rushed to Ron's side. "Ronald, you must come help."

"Marissa, meet my friends." He made quick introductions, explaining that Marissa owned the gallery.

"It's lovely to meet you. Thank you for coming,

but I must steal Ronald from you.'' She turned to Ron and grabbed his arm. ''Cecelia overheard some snide comment about one of the photographs—must have been some ignorant heathen who wandered in uninvited—and now she's locked herself in the bathroom and won't come out.''

Ron's shoulders heaved in defeat, as he again gazed longingly at Crystal. He turned back to Marissa. ''I'll be right there to see what I can do, but I'm not making any promises. The woman can be most stubborn.''

''Oh, thank you, dear. That's all I ask.'' Marissa wrung her bony hands. ''We can't very well have a showing without an artist.''

''I'll be back.'' With that, Ron turned to thread his way through the crowd.

''It's a lovely gallery,'' Crystal said to Marissa.

''Thank you, dear. You two make such a great-looking couple.'' She turned to Sam. ''You watch out for Ronald. I know how he operates. He'll steal this pretty thing from right under your nose or he'll at least try to.''

''I'll keep that in mind, ma'am.''

''You do that. Now, if you'll excuse me, I need to see to some champagne.''

The crowd shifted around them and Sam took Crystal's hand and pulled her into a quiet nook.

''What are we doing back here?'' she asked.

''Well, you could practice flirting or making Kincaid jealous.''

''But wouldn't it be better to do that in full sight? You know, where Ron is more likely to see us?''

He pulled her into his arms, pressing her hips close.

"Actually, this way he'll come looking for you and be all the more jealous when he sees I've got you in a compromising position."

"And how will you compromise me?"

"Like this." He lifted her chin and took her mouth, as he pulled her tightly against him.

He reveled in the feel of her body, the hungry sweep of her tongue as she kissed him back with the full force of her sensuality. The soft skin of her back teased his fingertips and he closed his eyes and pretended again that she was his. She moaned and moved against him, her breasts rubbing his chest, the V of her thighs cradling his burgeoning hard-on.

At long last, she pulled back. Her eyes glowed, a flush covered her cheeks and her lips seemed so round and inviting, it was all he could do not to drag her back for more. He took a deep breath. "You put my control to the test."

"Is that always so important to you?"

"What? Being in control?"

"Yes. You know what I think?"

"What?" He eyed her warily.

"I think you do everything you can to keep any serious emotions you might feel all bottled up inside you."

"Do I?"

"Yes, you do, and I think it is most unhealthy. Maybe this notion of yours to find a relationship of depth isn't such a bad idea."

"Well, I think it's unhealthy to get too involved in the wrong relationship."

"So how will you know when you find the right

relationship—when you've found someone you really care about and who cares about you?''

''I imagine I'll just know.''

''So, you're really going to give up all these hot and heavy physical relationships to leave yourself open for a possible relationship of the heart?''

''As I said, I'm going to give the physical relationships a break when you and I are through. Yes, I do realize there is something lacking in the purely physical. That's why I'm opening myself to something new, but unfortunately, I believe some people just are not meant to enjoy what you call relationships of the heart.''

''And you're not sure if you're one of those people?''

If only she could see Kincaid for the man he truly was, then she might put aside her foolish infatuation and realize that he, Sam, could give her just such a relationship. His chest swelled with the need to shake her and tell her, but an image of his father sitting drunk and dejected, forsaken by the woman he'd given his heart, swam before Sam's eyes.

Crystal would have to figure this one out on her own.

''Time will tell.''

Her eyes narrowed in speculation. ''And there's no chance you may have already stumbled on such a relationship?''

He let his gaze drift over her. Eye candy, she was certainly that now. But still not his. ''It doesn't appear so.''

She drew a breath and pushed away from him.

''Crystal—''

"Forget it. I don't know why I brought it up." She drew herself up and pasted on a smile. "I think I'll go mingle for a while. Maybe I'll see if I can find someone to practice flirting with."

"Well, you'd better come up with a better line than the one about him matching his clothes."

Crystal tossed her head and strode away into the crowd. Sam could be so infuriating. Maybe she wasn't the best flirt, but she was a good catch for the right man.

Was it not possible to have the best of both worlds, to have a great physical relationship as well as one of emotional depth? One didn't have to preclude the other. Did it?

"Hey there." Ron appeared at her side.

Her heart gave a jump. "Oh, hi. You surprised me. Aren't you on bathroom duty?"

"I talked her out." He nodded toward a salt-and-pepper-haired woman dressed as though she'd never escaped the sixties. A small crowd of admirers surrounded her as she gestured broadly to one of the life-size photos and spoke with much animation.

At least this woman didn't appear to be competition. "So, she's the famous artist."

"Here, I'll introduce you."

"No, that's okay. I wouldn't want to intrude. She seems to be on a roll."

He chuckled softly and it was a nice, warm sound that bubbled over her and brought a smile to her own face. "She'll be going all night. You know us artists," he said. "We love to talk about our work."

"So, you do consider yourself an artist?"

"Of course. Don't you?"

"I've never really thought of it that way. I suppose if I was writing fiction, but what I do... Well, I don't think anyone considers it art."

"Sure it is. Art is the creative process—in whatever medium you care to work in. You take a blank page or screen and you put words on it, right?"

"Right."

"You *create* the articles you write. That's art."

"If you say so."

"I do."

"Okay, then I'm an artist."

"Atta girl."

She grinned. This wasn't going so badly. Maybe she could try to flirt now. "Those are nice shoes."

His eyebrows arched. He glanced down at his feet. "Oh, thanks."

The musical notes of a cell phone sounded from his pocket. "Excuse me."

With the phone pressed to his ear, he moved away, then stopped and turned back.

"Hold on a sec," he said into the phone, then stepped back beside Crystal. "Would you be interested in coming by my photography studio this Tuesday afternoon to do a test shoot for an upcoming lingerie calendar?"

She stared at him, frozen in surprise.

He shrugged. "That's okay. I just thought I'd ask."

He'd turned away again, phone to his ear, before she found her voice. "Yes!"

"Hold on again," he said to whomever was on the line. He reached into another pocket, withdrawing a business card. "Here's the address. About three o'clock?"

"Sure." Her gaze drifted over the card, then back up to him.

"Great. See you then. Call me if you have any questions beforehand."

She nodded to his back as he melted again into the crowd, already deep in conversation with his caller.

9

SAM DREW A DEEP BREATH as he pulled into a parking spot outside Crystal's apartment. She'd been way too quiet on the ride home.

"He wants me to do a test shoot," she said without looking at him.

Sam's chest tightened. "Of course he does. When?"

"Tuesday afternoon."

Good. They had scheduled it for the same time as the board meeting. He'd need a major distraction. "Great. You'll do the shoot. He'll ask you out, then invite you to do the calendar. Mission accomplished."

Sam swallowed any regret and turned to face her. "So, have you come up with a topic for your first article?"

"For *Edge?*"

"Yes."

Pink tinged her cheeks and it was all he could do not to take her in his arms and let her know she'd be fine. She could write these articles, just as he could get on with life without her.

Somehow.

"I've been a little blocked," she said.

"Is that so?"

''I've been having a little trouble concentrating. With all this—'' she waved her hand ''—going on, it's been a little hard to focus.''

''What have you been working on?''

''I have this article due by Tuesday. It's about family reunions. It's a follow-up to that one I did last month on class reunions.''

''How's it going?''

''It's coming along. I've been interviewing different families and there's this one company that actually helps organize and plan different kinds of reunions. I'm working in a theme about keeping old traditions while bringing in new ones and how that can help family members gain fresh perspectives on their loved ones.''

''Sounds interesting.''

''I thought it was. And it is.'' She turned away, agitated. ''I haven't been able to finish it. I don't know what's wrong with me. I've been stuck since yesterday. I didn't write a thing last night, then hardly anything today. That just isn't like me—not when I'm on deadline.''

He did touch her then, taking her by her arms and turning her toward him. ''What's wrong, babe?''

''You know, you never called me that before...before we, you know.''

He loosened his grip, but couldn't bring himself to let go. She was upset about something and the need to fix it—make her world right again—overwhelmed him. ''Sure I did.''

Her gaze narrowed on him, accusing. ''No, you didn't. 'Honey,' 'sweetheart,' but never 'babe.'''

He dropped his hands. "I'm sorry. I won't call you that anymore."

A small growl escaped her. "That's not what I mean."

"Look, if it bothers you—"

"I just want to know what that means."

"What *what* means?"

"If I'm 'babe' to you now, when I wasn't before, what does that mean?"

The air around him seemed to thicken as he pulled it into his lungs. What exactly was she asking? "It's just a word, like 'honey' and 'sweetheart'."

"So they're interchangeable?"

He shrugged. "I guess."

Her eyes narrowed on him. "Did you call your other women 'babe' after you slept with them?"

"What?"

"I just want to know if this is a term of endearment you have assigned to me in particular since you started mentoring me or if it's just a reference you use for any woman you sleep with."

"It's just a word."

"You can be so annoying, Sam."

He drew back. "I'm sorry. I'm just not sure what you're asking."

"Forget it." She pulled her keys from her purse and jingled them in her hand. "Look, thanks for taking me tonight. It worked out really well."

She reached for the door handle.

"Stop."

"I should go in and try to work."

"Fine." He opened his door. "Stay put and let me get the door for you, then I'll walk you up."

"Okay."

She hardly spoke as they ascended the stairs to her apartment. When they reached her door, she stopped and smiled at him, though sadness clouded her eyes. It tore at him to see her anything less than happy.

He tilted her chin up. "Maybe if you tell me what's got you so upset, we can work out whatever it is."

"Oh, it's fine for me to talk about what I'm feeling, but not you?"

"Well, I'm feeling a little confused right now. How's that?"

She rolled her eyes. "Look, just forget it. I'm a little irritable with this deadline and everything."

"And maybe a little worried about Tuesday?"

"Maybe a little."

"You'll be sensational."

"Will you come?"

His gut clenched at the thought of watching her preen for Kincaid. "I've got a board meeting. It'll last the entire afternoon."

"Sure. I understand."

"I could help you tomorrow night, if you'd like. We can have you practice posing, get your attitude down."

"Would you like to come in now?"

His whole body seemed to sway involuntarily toward her, then he checked himself. "I think we should start weaning ourselves."

Her eyebrows arched in question.

"Kincaid won't make it through that test shoot without realizing what a catch you are. Tuesday's your day. You'll get the man of your dreams. And you won't need my mentoring services anymore."

"I don't know. I've got the feeling this test shoot is all business. He hardly spoke to me other than that. I don't think he's interested in anything personal. I just don't think I've caught his notice on that level."

"You've caught his interest. I'd bet on it. He's just a busy guy. Plus, he'll want the moment to be right before he makes his move." He cocked his head. "This arrangement of ours was always meant to be temporary. I think we should end it before the shoot."

"But, what if I do the test shoot and then nothing happens. I may never hear from him again."

"That isn't going to happen." He pulled her into his arms. "I know I've been tied up a lot lately, but we'll have all day and night Sunday. I have a late meeting Monday, but I'll come by as soon as we get done, maybe around eight or so, and we'll spend the entire evening together."

"Okay. I think I would like a practice shoot. I'll appreciate any pointers you want to toss my way."

He let his gaze travel her length. "You are so hot, all we'll be doing is fine-tuning. You'll be ready for Tuesday. I promise."

"Thanks, Sam." She tiptoed and kissed him good-night, just enough of a kiss to tempt him to stay. Then she pulled away and opened the door. "Sleep well."

"Sweet dreams."

He stood outside her door a moment after she'd gone inside. The chirping of the tree frogs around the lake welled up around him. She might be ready for Tuesday, but God help him, he would never be.

CRYSTAL GLARED AT THE STORM clouds scuttling overhead as she stomped back from her mailbox the following Monday afternoon. The weekend had been a bust. The Saturday game had been rained out, so she hadn't seen Ron. Then, though Sam had spent Sunday with her as promised, he'd been withdrawn and had to hurry off to a meeting this morning. She slammed the door shut, then kicked off her shoes and tore open a crisp envelope addressed in neat letters.

"A bridal shower?" She stared at the invitation, dismay filling her. What had Megs gotten herself into?

She punched her sister's work number into her phone, then waited, her foot tapping, until Megs picked up.

"Good afternoon, Margaret Peterson."

"All right, *Margaret,* when are you going to put an end to this farce?"

"Crystal, hi. Guess you got the invitation."

"You knew about this?"

"His sister e-mailed me the guest list to make sure she hadn't forgotten anyone."

"Megs."

"I tried to tell her, in a very diplomatic way, that you'd be upset, that you'd feel it was your place to throw the shower."

"Megs, have they brainwashed you?"

"I know, I know."

"Why haven't you talked to Leo?"

"You know…actually, we were lying there in bed the other night, just watching TV, like an old married couple and he passed gas and it didn't even faze me and he was perfectly at ease about it and I just thought… Well, we're so comfortable with each other."

"Megs—"

"No, I know what you're going to say, but I just think that maybe I could handle being married to Leo. His family adores me and he took me shopping yesterday and he wants to buy me a new car."

"Are you listening to yourself?"

"Yes, I'm saying I think I want to marry Leo."

"Because his family adores you, he's buying you a car and let's not forget that passing gas is a great experience for the two of you."

"Crystal—"

"Not once in that little speech did I hear anything remotely like, 'This is the man I am madly, deeply, never-going-to-fall-out-of-love-with, whose children I long to bear and raise and whose family I also love and adore more with each passing breath.'

"Very funny, now you're getting carried away, but I get your point."

"There just has to be more to a marriage than being comfortable with someone when they pass gas."

"Well, of course, but there's something there."

"I'm not saying there isn't, but is it enough? We're talking for the rest of your life, here. One man. This man. Is *he* the one?"

"Damn you, Crystal, why do you have to mess with my head like this?"

"Because I love you."

"Okay, I'll give it some more thought."

"Megs."

"What?"

"How would you feel if this situation were reversed and Leo was having doubts, but he didn't tell you?"

She was silent a moment, then said, "I guess I'd be mad and really hurt that he hadn't told me."

"Don't wait too long."

"I won't, and Crystal..."

"Yes?"

"Thanks."

"Sure, hon. Love you."

"I know. I love you, too."

"IT'S NOT WORTH IT." Cami pressed through her door early that evening and Crystal sighed. She only had another hour or so before Sam arrived. Guess her deadline would have to wait.

Not that today had been any more productive.

"What's not worth it?"

"This." Cami waved her hand over herself. "This whole makeover nonsense."

"Aw, hon, come on in. Can I get you anything?"

"Tequila?"

"How about a beer?"

"Sure, thanks."

She followed Crystal into her kitchen. "You were right."

"About what?"

"We didn't need these makeovers. At least, I didn't. I don't think you did, either, but you seem to have fared okay." She accepted the cold bottle, then took a long swig and trailed after Crystal into the living room.

"But the other day you were so happy about the new you. What's happened?" Crystal settled onto the sofa and Cami sank down beside her.

"Well, it seemed wonderful, at first. Everyone noticed me. I couldn't walk down the street without getting wolf calls and whistles. I know some women think it's obnoxious, but I was flattered. That's never happened to me before."

"That doesn't sound like such a bad thing."

"I didn't think so. And sometimes I'd even smile and wave back. No big deal. It wasn't like I started sleeping around or anything."

"Oh, dear, let me guess. This is all leading back to Parker."

"You wouldn't believe it, Crystal. I don't know who he is anymore. It's like some raving, jealous…insecure…monster has taken him over."

"I never thought he was the jealous type."

"He never was, but he never had anything to be jealous about before. Not that he does now.

"Okay, maybe I insisted we eat at Nava last night, instead of getting takeout like we usually do and maybe, just maybe, I drank a teensy weensy too much…"

"Uh oh."

"And it could be that I kind of sort of flirted with the waiter."

"Cami—"

"And the valet guy and…maybe, I think, with the maître d', too."

"So you flirted with a few guys. What's a little harmless flirting?"

"Then there's this guy at work."

Crystal took a long, fortifying swallow of her beer. "What guy?"

"He's new. Transferred from the Miami firm, deals mostly in domestic cases."

"And?"

Cami threw back her head and chugged half her beer. "I kissed him."

"You what?"

"Oh, God, I don't know how it happened."

"Does Parker know?"

"Like I would tell him."

"Well, how did it happen? Why?"

"Parker and I got into this huge fight after Nava last night and we fought again this morning. I was so mad at him for not trusting me. I couldn't understand how he could feel so threatened. Like any of these guys can hold a candle to him. I love him, Crys."

"Of course you do and he knows that. He's just having a little trouble adjusting to the new you and, evidently, you're having a little trouble adjusting, as well."

"There I was, in the copy room of all places, and the damn machine jammed and I couldn't get the paper out and I just started crying—over a stupid copier, though of course that was just the trigger. There I was, Niagara Falls, and in walks Ken—that's his name—and it was really early because I was so mad at Parker I just left this morning and no one else was around and Ken was so concerned and sweet and I just spilled my guts about all the trouble and the wolf calls and the flirting and I asked him if I was a bad girlfriend. And he started saying all these wonderful things about how beautiful I am and how he'd treat me if I was his girl and then I was just in his arms and he was looking at me like I was the most special person in the whole world, like he approved of me and liked me for who I was inside and then I kissed him."

"Wow."

"And then people started arriving at the office, so we broke it up and it's been horrendously awkward all day. And I don't know how I'm going to face Parker and look him in the eye...and I just feel horrible."

"Damn."

"Yeah."

"So, this guy, do you feel anything for him? Are you wanting to pursue a relationship with him?"

Cami's face screwed up in alarm. "No. Not at all. I don't know why I kissed him. It was a huge mistake."

"Right. Okay. And you still love Parker and want to be with him?"

"Oh, yes, more than ever. I hate fighting with him. I think...I think he was right. This whole makeover went to my head and I forgot for a bit about what's really important in life."

"Well, why can't you just tell him that?"

"You think I should clear the air, confess all, then start fresh?"

"Maybe. Will you lose him over that kiss?"

She considered, while she took another long swallow. "I honestly don't know, but I don't think I can live with it between us. I think I need to tell him, then accept the consequences."

A tear rolled down her cheek and Crystal reached over and hugged her. "It'll be all right."

"Oh, God, I hope so. I don't know what I'll do if I lose him."

"You're tough. You'll make it. But Parker is one smart cookie. He's not going to let a good thing go."

"You really think so?"

"Yeah, I do."

"Thanks." Cami straightened and wiped her eyes. "Maybe I should just go see him now and get it over with."

"Okay. I'll be here for you afterward, in case you need me."

"What would I ever do without you?" Cami gave her a long hug.

"Probably the same thing I would do without you—go stark raving mad or find another best friend and live happily ever after."

"Never. I couldn't bear it. You'll just have to accept that you're stuck with me for life."

"Sounds good to me." Crystal grinned broadly at her friend. "Now, go get him."

"Okay." Cami cocked her head. "So everything's all right with you? You're happy with your makeover? Everything's going well with your new dream man?"

"Oh, sure, Sam's fine."

"Sam?" Cami's eyebrows arched. "I was asking about Ron. So, you and Sam are officially on?"

Heat suffused Crystal's cheeks. Had she really said Sam? "No, nothing's changed between me and Sam. He's still just my…mentor—"

"Your *sexual* mentor. Hey, if you really don't want him and Parker blows me off, can I have Sam when you're through?"

A feeling of possessiveness rose up in Crystal.

"He's taking a break from women when we're done."

"You've ruined him for the rest of us."

"I have not. He's perfectly…functional."

"And you're in love with him. Admit it."

"I'll admit no such thing."

"But you just as well said he was your dream man a minute ago."

"I meant that Sam is a fine friend for helping to transform me, so I could snag Ron. Who, by the way, has asked me to come by his studio tomorrow afternoon to do a trial shoot for the lingerie calendar."

"Oh, good for you. But that story about Sam not being your dream man wouldn't even fool sweet Megs. I think we need to have a little discussion on this whole Sam-Ron issue."

"There is no Sam-Ron issue. And you have a much more important errand to run."

"It can wait. I'm guessing I'm not the only one who's been dealt a little makeover madness. Now, out with it."

"I'll make you a deal. If all goes well with Parker, we'll make a lunch date tomorrow and I'll tell you anything you want to know."

"Anything? Like where you got the tattoo, which I like, by the way."

"Anything."

"Okay, as long as you're really all right for now."

"I'm just peachy. Now, go."

"Fine. But we're on for lunch. We have to celebrate your trial shoot. If Ron really is the one you want, that's great progress. I have a good feeling about this. I say you'll get a spot in the calendar and you'll get the guy."

"Really?"

"Yeah, my guess is Sam will get so jealous, he'll confess his undying love."

"Would you just get out of here?"

"I'm gone."

Crystal stood on the porch long after Cami left. The night sounds emerged with the setting sun. She needed to get back to her article. With a sigh, she headed inside. Maybe Cami was right. Maybe Crystal had been struck by some makeover madness.

That might explain why she couldn't stop wondering what Sam was up to.

10

LIGHT SEEPED THROUGH the curtain on Crystal's front window, falling across the planks of her porch steps. Sam drew a deep breath and knocked on her door. Tonight would be his last night with her.

When her footsteps sounded from inside, he tightened his grip on the instant camera he'd brought. He wasn't much of a photographer, but if Crystal could see the pictures as they developed before her eyes, she might see how sexy she really was. He drew a deep breath. He had to hold himself together—resist the urge to drop to his knees and beg her to quit her plan to seduce Kincaid.

The door scraped open. She stood framed in the doorjamb, light spilling around her. A blue scrunchy held her hair in a mussed ponytail. She wore a loose T-shirt and boxers.

His heart quickened at the sight of her.

"Hello." She blinked, then stood staring at him another moment.

"Did I wake you?"

"No. I was actually working."

"So, can I come in?" He raised his eyebrows in question. He hadn't been able to get away from his dinner meeting as soon as he'd hoped. Had she forgotten their plans?

"Of course." She stepped back to let him enter, then closed the door behind him, her gaze swinging to the camera in his hand. "You brought a camera."

"It's time for your practice shoot." Damn, but she looked sexy, even in boxers—especially in boxers. "Ready?"

She glanced down at herself. "I'm not sure."

"No? Well, maybe we just need to get you in the mood."

He swept her into his arms. Before she could protest, his mouth closed over hers, his lips imploring her to open to him. She melted into his embrace and gave him all he asked and more, her tongue mating hungrily with his and her fingers tangling in his hair, plucking at the buttons of his shirt.

"Sweetheart," he murmured, when he at last drew back, "I have been looking forward to that the entire day."

"Me, too. I'm sorry I'm not quite ready." She gestured to her attire.

He turned her toward her bedroom. "I see you've been backsliding. Not that I'm complaining." He ran his hand over her boxer-clad bottom.

She turned to him, pink flooding her cheeks. "Something tells me I could wear a burlap bag and you wouldn't complain."

"Ah, but it isn't what *I* approve of that matters, is it?" He clenched his jaw against a wave of regret.

"Well, I suppose I'm not looking for your personal approval then, but your professional endorsement would be much appreciated."

He took a deep breath and guided her to the bed.

“Time to play dress up. Sit here and get comfortable. Where’s your lingerie?”

“There—” she pointed “—top drawer. So, you actually want to take pictures?”

“I figure a practice run won’t hurt—get you used to being in the spotlight.” After setting the camera on the dresser, he opened the drawer to find the plunder from their shopping spree at Secret Temptations.

“Let’s start...with...this.” He pulled out the peach-colored teddy. “Sit up. Raise your arms.”

She did as he instructed and he slipped off her T-shirt. Her sports bra followed. He bent to kiss her and caress her breasts, his thumbs stroking her nipples into taut beads, then he shook his head over her boxers. “Seems a shame to lose these.” He sighed a dramatic sigh. “But I guess they’ll have to go.”

Gently, he rolled her to her back, then pulled the soft cotton off her hips, down her legs, taking extra care not to disturb her tattoo, then over her feet, to discard the garment on the floor with the rest of her clothes. She lay naked, her forehead furrowed, her lower lip trapped between her white teeth. He drank in her every line and curve as the bedside light played over her soft skin.

“I just needed to be comfortable today,” she said, her voice pitched a little high.

Could she be nervous around him still, after all they’d been through? The thought sent warmth expanding in his chest. He sank to the bed beside her.

“I’ve been working—writing nonstop, finally,” she continued. “I have the reunion article nearly finished. I promise I’ll brainstorm ideas for *Edge* before I start on the first makeover piece.”

"Good." He smoothed his hand along the soft curve of her stomach. His blood warmed as she sat up, then stretched her arms again over her head, waiting for him to slip on the teddy.

"I don't know." He again let his gaze slide over her as he cupped one perfect breast. "I kind of like you this way."

She dropped her arms. "You are *not* taking naked pictures of me."

"Very well." He slid the teddy over her head, threaded her arms through the thin straps, then tugged the garment down over her body, smoothing the lacy fabric along her breasts, stomach and hips.

His pulse thrummed as his gaze fell on the rise and fall of her breasts. "Relax, Crystal, lie back."

She slipped back onto the bed and bent one knee as he reached for the snaps between her legs. His cock stirred at the sight of her mons and he hesitated a long moment, while he feasted his eyes on her sweet treasure.

"Maybe we should leave this unsnapped a minute." He ran his fingers over her springy curls to where her sex beckoned him.

Her eyes grew dark and a small moan escaped her as he traced her thick folds. God, she was beautiful, so beautiful. And she was already wet for him. He pressed his fingers against her entrance.

"Wait. Sam, don't."

"No?" It was all he could do not to slip his fingers inside her. She was so hot. Her pulse throbbed beneath his hand. She wanted him.

"The pictures. We're getting sidetracked." She scooted away from him, then busied herself with the snaps. She rose to her knees, brushing up against him. "I promise later, we'll do whatever you want."

He exhaled. He'd already forgotten about the damn camera. "You're right. You do distract me."

Tamping down on his desire, he brushed a kiss over her forehead, then moved away from her to retrieve the Instamatic. "I should probably keep my distance for this. Stay back, where I can't touch you."

She nodded and licked her lips. Then she blew out a long breath. "Okay, I can do this."

He raised the camera to his eye, then lowered it. "Hold on."

"What?"

"Your hair." He set the camera down, then approached her, his hands raised. "I'm just going to touch your hair, nothing else."

"Oh...fine." She stilled as he freed her silky locks from the scrunchy.

Eyes closed, he inhaled the clean scent drifting from her hair. His fingers sank into the soft strands and she rolled her head as he massaged her scalp. Another small moan escaped her and his groin tightened.

Damn if he wasn't getting turned on just by touching her head.

"Hold that look." He grabbed the camera, then focused through the lens. Her head tilted back, her eyes closed, a dreamy expression covered her face. He snapped the picture, then tossed the developing image on the dresser, without looking at it. "That was good. Now, try something else."

She straightened and stared at him. The dreamy

look left her and she again caught her lower lip in her teeth. "I don't know. I feel so awkward."

"Forget I have the camera. It's attitude, remember. Think about your body language. You liked when I was just touching you earlier, right? How did it feel to have me stroking you so intimately?"

Her gaze heated. "It made me hot."

"That's it." He snapped another picture, then laid it beside its comrade, frowning at the half-developed picture. He'd cut off the top of her head. Shaking his own head, he focused again on Crystal. "Show me you want me."

She leaned toward him, her breasts shifting in the lacy bodice. "I want you, Sam."

"Don't tell me. Show me."

Her spine arched as she jutted her breasts forward as if she offered them for his pleasure. The shutter again whirred and he closed his eyes, fighting the temptation to forget the pictures and jump her.

A soft moan drew his attention back to her. She had stretched on her side on the bed, her top knee bent just enough to show the shadow of her sex beneath the lace. The fingers of one hand traced the edge of the teddy along one cup that hugged her breast. She wet her lips and gave him the most "come hither" look he'd ever witnessed.

He swallowed hard, snapped one last picture, then tossed the camera onto the dresser. In one motion, he pounced on her, pulling her hot body up hard against his and claiming her mouth with an insistence he couldn't contain.

She went wild in his arms, tugging at his shirt until she'd freed him from it, then tossing it to the floor, all the while kissing him with a force he was more than willing to reckon with. Her mouth left his to trail over his chest, across his nipples, then down his stomach.

When her fingers curled around his belt buckle, he gritted his teeth and pulled her upward. "Whoa. We need to slow down. Let me love you, first."

She gazed at him, her eyes glazed with passion. "Okay, you call the shots."

His hands shook slightly as he combed his fingers through his hair and tried to calm his racing heart. "I just want to love you all night. I need to pace myself."

Nodding, she settled back and closed her eyes, her breasts rising and falling with her breath. "I'm sorry. You just make me want you so bad."

He basked for a moment in her words, in the sight of her, then he again pulled her to him and slid one strap off her shoulder, over her arm, freeing her luscious breast. As he kissed her there, she clasped his head to her. He laved her nipple, while kneading its firm twin. Nothing had ever tasted sweeter. He drew on her for long moments and her fingers threaded through his hair.

While the pressure in his groin increased, he kissed his way down her lace-covered torso, settling between her legs. He nuzzled the apex of her thighs, breathing deeply of her heady scent. He undid his own belt then and loosened his slacks, while he committed each sigh, each flash of desire in her eyes to memory.

"Open for me, babe. Show me how much you want me."

She drew her knees up, one arched foot grazing his shoulder. Her eyes implored him. "Sam..."

The snaps parted with the flick of his wrist. He pushed aside the flimsy lace, then hesitated for a moment, etching the sight of her arousal in his mind, before lowering his mouth to her. He took his time, kissing her with slow strokes of his tongue, memorizing the taste and feel of her for the long nights ahead.

"Oh, God, Sam," her voice came halting, breathless. "I want...I want to kiss you, too."

She reached for him, tried to tug him around. He lifted his head and his gaze met hers. Heat and desire flowed between them. This time, when her fingers found his waistband, he let her have her way. In a moment he stood before her, free of the confining clothes.

She pressed up against him and kissed him, her tongue dueling with his. Could she taste herself? Did she like it as much as he did?

After a moment, she pulled back, her pupils dilated, her face flushed. He settled back on the bed. "Now, where were we?"

The pink in her cheeks deepened. "You were kissing me and you were going to let me kiss you, too."

"Yes." He crooked his finger. "Come here."

She moved beside him. He lifted her by her waist, and she gasped as he turned her, then set her down, so her knees straddled his head. "Right where I want you," he said, stroking her hips and gazing up at her flesh, swollen with his loving.

"Oohh..." The sound ended in a moan as he

pulled her to his mouth and kissed her, drinking in her liquid desire.

At first she rocked against him, seemingly lost in the sensations he stirred, then her weight came down over him, her soft body pressing into his as her hands closed over his erection. A shudder ran through him, when her sweet lips touched him. She kissed him as she'd done before, tracing his length from base to tip, holding him, stroking him, then finally taking him into her mouth.

He endured the intense sensations she granted him for as long as he dared, then he focused on her pleasure, distracting her with the steady flick of his tongue, the grating of his teeth against her sensitive flesh. Her grip on his cock loosened and her mouth left him as she became caught up in his ministrations.

Excited cries tore from her. He slipped two fingers inside, strumming her tight passage as she moaned and arched up over him. Her hips undulated and she met him as he thrust into her. He closed his eyes, focusing on her movements, her soft cries, the tensing of her muscles as her climax approached.

He read the language of her body and responded in kind, bringing her to fulfillment. She stiffened and emitted one last, drawn-out cry as the orgasm took her. He slowed his loving, laving her gently, until she lay still on top of him.

Then she must have remembered what she'd been about and her hand again closed over his cock, now hard and throbbing. She stroked and kissed him, while he gritted his teeth and gripped her buttocks. When he feared he'd lose control, he lifted her, settling her beside him. She let him go with a reluctant groan and he nearly came anyway at the hungry look in her eyes.

"Babe, when I come, I want to be deep inside you," he managed, though it was hard to breathe, let alone speak.

"Well, then..." She smiled a knowing smile as she opened her nightstand drawer, then withdrew a condom.

He collapsed on the pillows and let her ready him. Then she stretched out on top of him and kissed him long and hard. He rolled her to her back and she opened to him, guiding him to her slick entrance. He knew heaven as he slid into her welcoming heat. He let the sensations take him, loving her repeatedly through the night. When he came deep inside her for the last time in the early-morning light, he did so with his body and all of his heart.

BUTTERFLIES STORMED Crystal's stomach as she pushed through a glass door emblazoned with the bold lettering *Ron Kincaid Photography.* A chime announcing her entry sounded like an alarm in her head. Her stomach clenched. She hadn't been able to reach Cami about lunch and Sam had seemed as if he was saying goodbye for good when he'd left that morning. She felt as though she was completely alone and unprepared.

Shaking off a feeling of impending doom, she pushed past the reception area as Ron had instructed when she'd called that morning to confirm their appointment. Photographs of gorgeous strangers with perfect smiles and flawless skin stared intimidatingly down at her from one wall. She straightened her shoulders and hurried past.

"Crystal, there you are." Ron emerged from behind a curtain to one side of an open area.

A large backdrop dominated one wall and various light fixtures were suspended from the ceiling, along tracks or stood independently about the floor.

She shielded her eyes against one of the lights and forced a smile, though her stomach churned so badly she feared she might be ill. What was she doing here? Competing against professional models for a coveted spot in a calendar? Had she lost her mind?

"You look great. You ready for this?"

"I don't know." She clutched the strap on her bag. If only Sam had been able to join them. She could have used his moral support.

"Why don't you just take a deep breath and relax? You'll be fine."

She dragged in a couple of lungfuls of air and did her best to loosen her muscles, but it seemed her entire body tensed right up again. "I'm a little nervous."

"Tell you what, we won't start until you feel at ease and comfortable with everything. Why don't we try some mellow music?"

She nodded. "That would be nice."

He left her for a moment, then shortly afterward sultry jazz tones wavered in the air. She closed her eyes and focused on the forlorn notes, while breathing slow, deliberate breaths. When she opened her eyes, Ron stood before her, his gaze soft and intent.

"Better?" he asked.

"Yes, I think so."

"Great. Here, let me show you the dressing area. I've put a number of garments back here you may like to try." His gaze assessed her from head to toe, then back again. "I think I've got the right size, but let me know if not or if you don't find anything you like. I have a small supply of lingerie, though nothing like the spread we'll have when we do the actual calendar."

She nodded, not sure what to say or do with herself. It seemed she'd planned so long for this event and now that it was here she couldn't quite bring herself to enjoy it. Whatever was wrong with her?

"Come along, then." He grabbed her hand and towed her toward the curtained area.

They pushed through the drapes into a softly lit room. A mirrored vanity resided along one wall and a clothing rack stood before a floor-to-ceiling mirror. A rainbow assortment of lingerie filled the rack.

Ron dropped her hand and turned to her. "Would you like a glass of wine, beer, something to help you relax?

"No, thank you."

"Would you like me to help you choose something or would you rather I left you to try things on your own?"

The memory of her dressing-room encounter with Sam washed over her and she warmed. "I think I would rather try things on my own."

"Okay. I'm going to go play with the lighting, then. Just come on out when you find something you like and we'll see what happens."

She nodded and smiled nervously as he backed out through the curtains. Swallowing, she dropped her bag and turned to the rack. Panic welled up inside her as she eyed the soft fabrics and sheer pieces. She lifted a baby-blue bustier, with matching lace G-string off the rack. It would match her butterfly. She glanced down at her ankle. The tattoo was healing nicely, though her pulse seemed to throb beneath the delicate wings.

What was she doing here? She hardly knew Ron. Was she really about to parade herself in front of him, wearing one of these body-revealing outfits? And if she was nervous about having one man see her, how would she feel if she actually landed a spot in the calendar for who knows how many men to view?

You don't worry about what anyone thinks. It shows a certain confidence.

Sam's words rang clearly in her mind. She straightened and turned to the mirror, her head high. He may have been referring to her sweats and T-shirts at the time, but there was no reason why her attitude had to change with her clothes.

"I can do this."

She quickly slipped off her outfit, then stepped into the bustier and G-string. She eyed a matching garter and stockings, but decided against them. If she took much longer, she might lose her nerve.

After a quick check in the mirror, she pushed through the curtain. The strains of the saxophone floated over her as she padded to the lighted area, where Ron fidgeted with a camera on a tripod. A second camera hung from his neck.

He straightened, turning toward her, a slow smile dawning across his lips. "Nice choice. Sexy and sophisticated. I like it."

She spread her arms and made a slow turn in front of him, closing her eyes and imagining Sam's green gaze on her. When she opened her eyes again, Ron already had the camera poised. The soft click of the shutter sounded in a break of the music, sending flutters through her stomach. She lifted her chin, though, and moved toward the backdrop where he'd arranged an assortment of large pillows.

Good, she could pretend she was home in her living room...and Sam was with her, watching her, making love to her. Warmth spread over her as she let memories from the previous night drift through her mind: Sam with his hungry kiss and urgent hands; his strong body covering her, moving her to heights she'd never before explored; his beautiful face frozen in a look of pure ecstasy.

"God, this is incredible."

Ron's voice drew her back to the present. The clicking of the camera's shutter was barely distinguishable above the music. She smiled at the photographer. She was here for him and she had his full attention, just as she'd planned.

"That's good. Oh, but you're a natural." He moved in closer and glanced up from the camera. "Wet your lips. Now, toss your hair back. Good. Good."

Crystal, you take my breath away.

Sam's words flowed over her, igniting a feeling of power and feminine pride. She shook out her hair and let the feeling take her. Focusing on Ron, she channeled this energy into every movement.

He continued to talk, his voice encouraging and approving. Yet, a deeper baritone played in her head.

Sam murmuring soft words in her ear as his body stroked hers, arousing her beyond reason.

Sweetheart, do you know how much I want you?

Taking a slow breath, she let her gaze assess Ron, who still stood godlike in his golden glory. As his eyes heated with definite desire, the truth dawned in a moment of clarity, blowing away the confusion of the past week.

She looked at Ron and felt…nothing. No tingling running up and down her spine, no warmth spreading from her middle, no excitement at the possibilities of this afternoon alone with him.

With this realization came a profound understanding. Sam wanted her, really wanted her—not just for the physical release she granted him, but for the fuller meaning she could bring into his life. This understanding came from the memories of her body, of his tender loving that spoke of the emotion he kept locked inside. He may not yet realize how deep his feelings ran—may not be able to express in words how he cared for her—but she knew with the certainty of her heart that the truth lay in his lovemaking.

Only then did he let his guard down.

She tossed back her head and let joy burst through her. And more, she wanted him, too, with every fiber of her being. By night's end Sam would be hers. She closed her eyes, basking in her revelation, her entire body tingling with excitement. Could this be love?

11

SAM SETTLED BACK in the leather chair and nodded as his father entered the boardroom. He strode with the same confidence he always had, as though he owned the place. Only a practiced eye could discern the effort each movement cost him. Half a dozen greetings met him at once and he acknowledged each, shaking hands and exchanging pleasantries as he made his way to his seat across from Sam.

"Sam, I trust you didn't make everyone wait for me, did you, son?"

"No, sir. I think Percy was just getting ready to drop that gavel, with or without you."

Percy Donaldson shook his stout finger at Sam. "Now, don't go getting me in trouble with the man." He turned to Sam's father. "You ready, Robert? I wouldn't dream of starting without you."

Robert picked up an agenda from the massive mahogany conference table and waved Percy on. "Let's get this show on the road. The sun's shining and I'd like to get a little golf in this afternoon."

Percy hefted his gavel, bringing it down with a quick rap. "You heard the man. This board meeting is now called to order. Everyone listen up."

Sitting through the reading of the minutes had always been a challenge for Sam. This afternoon it proved harder than usual. Thoughts of Crystal distracted him at every moment.

How was the trial shoot going? Was she heating up Kincaid's studio the way she'd heated up Sam's car the other night? God, he hoped not.

Was Kincaid maintaining a professional atmosphere or had he given in to her game of seduction? Sam clenched his pen and blotted the thought from his mind. He'd go insane if he thought about Crystal and the photographer together.

"What do you think, Sam?" Percy watched him, his eyes rounded in question.

"Sir?"

"We're discussing the merits and challenges of moving the office."

Sam fought to focus on the discussion at hand. "I'd say a poll of all employees is called for before we make any decisions."

His father grunted in dissent across the table. "I don't think this is a decision we need to open to anyone beyond the board. We have the capacity to make this decision now and roll it out over the next few months."

"I disagree." Sam leaned forward, his gaze intent on his father. "A change like this, especially with the potential of downsizing like we discussed, needs to be done with full communication. We need to consider employee morale. If we include them in the decision-making process—give them a choice—we'll take less of a hit in that area."

"He has a point," John Simms, one of the directors, said. "And we don't want to lose anyone to a longer commute. I think we'd be well served by a survey.''

Robert shook his head. ''If we don't move on something soon, we may lose the space we're currently interested in.''

''Better to lose the space than lose the people.'' Sam kept his gaze steady on his father who sat stiff in his seat.

Simms cleared his throat. ''I move we form a committee to draw up a survey and administer it to all employees.''

The motion was seconded and passed, Robert assenting in the face of an overwhelming majority. Sam volunteered to draw up the survey as his father looked on with disapproval. The rest of the meeting seemed to go downhill from there. The afternoon dragged on. Sam butted heads with his father over the advertising budget, then the new cover design Sam had had a committee study and create.

It was a relief when Percy finally adjourned the meeting and the members slowly filed out, their parting conversations subdued under the tension emanating from where Sam remained, facing his father. His father sat dark and frowning, his fingers steepled as the last of the board members left, closing the door behind him.

''What has gotten into you, son? I thought we talked about this. You don't want to mess with proven success.'' Robert pressed his hands flat on the table, a sign of his effort to contain his temper.

Sam tamped down on his growing anger. Did he have to fight for every bit of autonomy? ''We did talk about this and I still think some change is a good thing.''

''I don't know who you are anymore.'' With a scrape of his chair, his father moved back from the table.

''Wait, Dad, let's discuss this.''

Robert stood, glaring down at him. ''There will be no further discussion. I'll remind you I still have controlling interest in this magazine and as long as I do, we will run things my way.''

As he stormed from the room, Sam crumpled the meeting's agenda. So much for the National Magazine Awards and, of course, the controlling interest. He'd have to find some way to patch things up with his father, while helping him to see that the changes Sam proposed would only better the magazine.

Maybe once his father read Crystal's column, he'd come around. Even though Crystal hadn't started on an article, Sam knew she wouldn't let him down. He'd readied her for Kincaid, now it was time for her to uphold her end of their bargain.

THE BLINKING MESSAGE indicator on Crystal's answering machine beckoned as she slipped inside her door later that afternoon. She smiled. Had Sam called to ask how the shoot had gone?

What would she tell him? Should she confront him with her realization that they were meant for a serious relationship? Maybe she'd just tell him she'd changed her mind about Ron, that Sam made a better lover. Then she'd let him eventually come to his own conclusions. How much longer could the man live in denial?

Under her short skirt and clingy top, she still wore the bustier and G-string. Ron had insisted she keep them, convincing her to put on the garter and stockings for a few final shots. She couldn't wait for Sam to see her in her new regalia. Tonight she'd focus all her attention on him, let him know, if not in words then with her body, that he rocked her universe.

A giddy feeling took over her and she laughed out loud as she pressed the message button on her answering machine. The tape whirred, but no message played. Frowning, she checked the volume, then shook her head as she slid the control higher. Not wanting to be disturbed, she'd turned off the ringer on her phone and lowered the volume on her answering machine yesterday, when she'd finally gotten on a writing roll.

"Crystal?" Cami's choked voice sounded over the machine and Crystal tensed. Cami. God, when had she called?

"Crystal, where are you?" Her words faded into a sob and Crystal's stomach tightened. "I...I can't breathe. He left. Shit, he was so angry. What am I supposed to do? I'm...I'm home."

The message ended and Crystal stood staring as the tape reset. Had Cami called last night, while Crystal had been with Sam? She whipped the phone off the hook and punched in Cami's number, a feeling of dread stealing over her. How could she have let Cami down like that?

After four rings Cami's voice mail picked up and Parker's mellow baritone voiced a recorded message, sounding for all the world as though nothing were wrong. Crystal slammed down the phone, then dialed

Cami's work number. She twisted the phone cord around her finger as the line rang into the message center.

"Cami, this is Crystal. I'm so sorry. I forgot I had my ringer off." God, she sounded lame. "I'm so, so sorry. I'm here now. It's almost five. Call me."

She left a similar message on Cami's cell, then broke the connection. Slowly, she sank to the couch. What to do?

The sudden peal of her phone had her jumping. She grabbed the receiver, but dropped it on the floor in her haste. Swearing under her breath, she fumbled the phone to her ear. "Hello?"

"Crystal." Her mother's shaky voice sounded over a static-filled line. "Thank…God you answered the… phone. I've been calling and…calling."

"Mom, what's wrong?"

"Where's Megs? I need your sister. Where is she?" Panic tinged her words.

"I don't know. I haven't seen her today. She doesn't answer her cell phone?"

"No." A loud sob escaped her.

Crystal's anxiety level rose. Something was terribly wrong. "Are you home? Where's Dad?"

"Your father…" The sobbing broke out in earnest.

"Has something happened to Dad?" Her heart pounded in her ears. "Mom? Talk to me."

"How could he do this to me? I need your sister, she can talk some sense into him."

"What did he do?"

"He's ruined everything."

"Look, I'm coming over, okay?"

"Okay."

The helplessness in her mother's voice propelled Crystal out the door.

"HOW COULD YOU DO THIS?" Hurt and betrayal filled Crystal's mother's voice as it rang through the old house.

Crystal pushed through the screen door, then followed her mother's sobs and her father's muffled pleas to their back bedroom.

Damn, why hadn't Megs been home? This was more her area of expertise. Crystal hesitated as she neared the open door. Maybe she shouldn't intrude. Let her parents work this out on their own.

"For God's sake, Sarah, you called Crystal?" Bob Peterson, Crystal's father, stood in the open doorway, shaking his shaggy head.

"Someone has to talk some sense into you." Her mother grabbed Crystal by the arm, dragging her into the room.

"This isn't necessary." Her father's voice held a note of desperation and Crystal's heart swelled for him.

"Dad, what is it? What's happened?" she asked.

"I told you what's happened," her mother answered, still holding tight to her arm. "He's ruined everything. That's what's happened."

"Dad?"

"I quit my job."

Crystal stared at him for a long moment, stunned. "You what?"

"I quit my job. I am no longer the vice president of finance at Manning Health Care." He stood straight and tall, his chin raised high.

''I told you. He's ruined everything,'' her mother wailed. She finally released Crystal to cradle her face in her hands as she sobbed uncontrollably.

Deep grooves formed between her father's eyebrows. The weight of the world seemed to settle over her father. He sank to the bed. ''I'll get another job. I'll find a way to get the house.''

''How?'' Sarah raised her head and stared at him, her eyes wide and red rimmed. ''It took you ten years to land that promotion, then you threw it all away in a month's time. Who's going to hire you after that?'' She spread her arms wide. ''How will we even keep *this* place, now?''

''Mom, it'll be all right.'' Crystal wished desperately for Megs.

Her sister would know exactly the right thing to say and do. Megs had always been the sensible one, the peacemaker. This was the worst time ever for her to go MIA.

As her mother dissolved into tears and crumpled into a chair, Crystal settled beside her father on the bed. She squeezed his hand as he stared ahead blankly. ''Talk to me.''

He turned to her and blinked. ''I'll find a way. She deserves that house. I want her to have it, with all the trimmings—the new carpet and drapes, the gazebo and the country club. I'll get it for her. I will.''

''I know you will. What happened at work?''

His shoulders heaved as he drew a tired breath. ''I tried, honey. Really I did.''

''I know you did.'' She patted his hand. ''Tell me about it.''

''The corporate office is a whole new ball field—

not like the facilities. My time just wasn't my own. I had all this work to do and no time. Every minute was eaten up with meetings and conference calls. Everyone's in crisis. Everyone needs the reports I haven't completed, because I'm too busy putting out fires I didn't start. I felt so damn incompetent. I couldn't function."

He rose to pace along the threadbare carpet. "And not a resident in sight." He shook his head. "I think they forget in corporate what we're really about. That the Mrs. Finleys and the Joseph Murdocks are the ones who really need us. That all the residents who come to us for long-term care are our top priority. Real people with real needs. Everything we do should be geared toward that. We can't make budget cuts that affect that care."

He closed his eyes as if pained. "It just sickened me."

"You'll call Mr. Bannon, tell him you're sorry. He'll take you back. They couldn't have found a new VP already." Sarah clutched his hand.

"You're not hearing me, dearest. I was boxed in. I couldn't breathe there. I can't go back."

"Mom—" Crystal took her mother by the shoulders. "Let's go make some tea."

"Tea? How will that help?"

"It'll make you feel better. We'll have some tea. We'll talk. We'll figure out a plan."

"The plan is you're going to talk some sense into your father. He has to go back."

"But why? If he was so unhappy, why is that the only option?" Crystal's gaze swung from her mother to her father. Yesterday, they'd been on their way to paradise. How had things gotten so messed up?

"So my happiness counts for nothing?"

"Of course it counts." Her father frowned his disapproval and motioned Crystal away from her mother.

She stepped back as he swept his arm around her mother's shoulder. "We'll work it out."

"No." She pushed away from him. "If you really cared about my happiness, you'd go back. You can work things out with your boss, learn how to cope with your new environment. I don't see how it's so different from your job as regional controller."

"Damn it, woman, listen to me."

"I will not listen to you when you use that foul language. No more discussion." She waved her hands as though fending them both off, then grabbed her purse from the dresser.

"Where are you going?" Crystal's father asked as her mother moved down the hall.

"Away from people who swear at me and put their happiness over mine."

He clenched his hands, his face dark with anger. "Go ahead and leave then." His gaze swept to Crystal. "Both of you."

Crystal turned to him. "Dad—"

"Just go!"

Frustration welled in her and tears swam in her eyes. She turned her back on the man who had raised her and headed after her mother.

CLOUDS MOVED ACROSS what little moon shone down on the house Megs rented with Jules and another girl Crystal never saw enough of to remember. Crystal exited her car, then headed up the front walk. A moth flapped wildly around the light hanging beside the faded front door.

Raised voices sounded from inside and angry footsteps pounded in her direction. She stopped on the bottom step as the door yanked open. Leo stood frozen in the doorway, his face dark with anger.

"You..." He pointed an accusing finger in her direction, his black eyes snapping. "This is your doing, isn't it?"

"What?"

Megs appeared in the door behind him. "Leo, wait. Don't go away like this. Let's talk this out."

"Talk?" A note of hysteria tinged his laugh. "I think you've said all I need to hear." His eyes narrowed on Crystal. "They were her words, right? She's the writer, isn't she? Did she help you write out a practice speech?"

"Now, wait a minute—" Crystal started.

"They were my words," Megs spoke over her.

Leo pushed through the door, then paused on the front step, turning toward Megs. When he spoke, some of his anger seemed to have drained from him and his voice took on a defeated tone. "I would have given you everything."

"Leo..." Tears streamed down her sister's face. She reached for him, but he jerked away, then descended the stairs two at a time, brushing by Crystal without a word.

Megs started down after him, but Crystal stopped her. "No, let him go. He'll be all right."

"Will he?" The whites in Megs's eyes showed as

she slumped down onto the top step. "And what about me?"

"Oh, sweetie, you'll be okay, too. I take it you called off the wedding." Crystal settled beside her sister, scooping a comforting arm around her.

Megs nodded, then dropped her head onto her folded arms. Her shoulders shook with her silent tears.

Who had declared it national turmoil day? Crystal closed her eyes, feeling more tired than she ever had in her life. She had hurried after her mother, who'd driven off by the time Crystal had reached her car. She'd lost her when Sarah swerved into a far lane, then turned at a light. After searching all the places Crystal thought she might be to no avail, she had headed to her sister's, hoping Megs would be able to help.

She shook her head. Megs had enough on her plate for now. Crystal couldn't burden her with the news that their parents had gone off the deep end.

Megs straightened suddenly and moved away from Crystal. "Why did I have to listen to *you?*"

"Megs—"

"I've made a terrible mistake. Everything was fine until I started listening to you. Why did you have to spoil everything? You just couldn't take that I was happy and you…you didn't have anyone."

Crystal stared, openmouthed at her sister. Where had this come from?

Megs swiped at the tears running down her cheeks. "I used to be so jealous of you. You were always so sure of yourself, but look at you." She gestured to the short skirt and body-hugging top Crystal wore.

"You've made yourself into something you're not just to get the attention of some guy who'd never want anything more than to get into your pants."

Megs turned then ran back into the house, slamming the door behind her. Crystal stared out into the night and let her own tears streak down her face.

12

"COME ON, CAMI, ANSWER." Crystal leaned her head back against her couch a short while later and closed her eyes, when Cami's voice mail picked up.

She left another message. She'd called everyone she could think of, but no one had seen or heard from Cami. Where was she?

Crystal ground her teeth, frustration welling up inside her. Maybe she should drive by Cami's, see if her friend was home and just not answering the phone.

"Well, I can't sit here, waiting," she said to her silent walls.

She was too anxious to work and too nervous to sit still. With a determined step, she whisked her purse from the coffee table, then headed again out her door.

How had her day taken such a bad turn?

Fifteen minutes later, she pulled up to the town house Cami shared with Parker. The driveway stood empty; the windows yawned dark and lifeless. Frustration filling her, Crystal stepped from her car, then moved slowly up the brick-lined walk to the house.

The place appeared deserted. What she would do if Parker answered the door, she couldn't say, but she had to give it a try. She rang the bell four times for good measure, waiting patiently after each ring, straining to hear any faint stirrings from inside.

"Where are you, Cam?"

Distressed, Crystal headed back to her car. She'd been on the road for a good ten minutes before she straightened at the sight of the exit marker on the interstate. She'd missed her turn. In two exits she'd be near Sam's.

Sam. Just the thought of him warmed her.

Perhaps her subconscious had led her here, her unspoken need to be near him—to bask in his strength and comfort. What if he was busy? What if he wasn't home? She drew a deep breath and squelched all the questions swirling through her mind.

What harm would it do to drive by and see if he was in? If he wasn't, she could always see him tomorrow. And if he was...well the drive would be worth it just to have his arms around her.

Not long afterward, she stood on his doorstep. A breeze whipped up her skirt and she smoothed it down, her hands tracing the outline of the bustier and garter she still wore under her street clothes. In spite of her concern over her family and Cami, a little thrill ran through her.

No matter what the day had brought, here she'd find peace and fulfillment with Sam. She pressed the doorbell, then closed her eyes as his footsteps drew near. Surely, he'd be pleased to see her.

The door scraped open and he stood in his darkened entryway, his expression unreadable. "Crystal. What brings you here?"

Her heart sank at his lack of enthusiasm, but he did care for her, no matter how he chose to hide it. She had to hold on to that certainty. She lifted her chin. "Why, *you* bring me here."

He stared at her a moment, then stepped back and gestured for her to enter. "I thought you'd be off enjoying yourself with Kincaid."

"We ended the shoot hours ago." She stepped inside, her arms spread wide. "Don't I get a hug?"

He hesitated for just a moment, then wrapped her in his embrace. Doubt weighed his tone as he said, "And he didn't ask you out afterward?"

She drew back. "Actually, I've had second thoughts about Ron."

Ron had indeed asked her to dinner, but she'd declined, saying she had plans. At the time she did have plans to come seduce Sam. She was a little late carrying it out, but as his stance relaxed, she took heart that she might salvage this night, after all.

Sam breathed in the sweet scent of her, surprised, but wary of her appearance on his doorstep. "What do you mean?"

"I've had a rough night. I can't find Cami. She and Parker are having problems. My parents had a major blowup. Megs blames me for ruining her life and I just wanted to be with you." She pressed her body again close to his, her arms still looped loosely around his neck. Her soft lips caressed his ear.

"Crystal..." Though his body protested, he pulled her arms free, disappointment tightening his gut. She'd had a rough night and she'd come for comfort sex. Was that the role she wished for him now?

"What's the matter, Sam?" The gentle tone of her voice nearly melted his resolve. "Here, there's something I want to show you."

She moved away from him into the living room where light from a side table cast a soft glow over her. She dropped her purse on the oversize lounger she'd talked him into buying years ago. A slow smile curved her lips as she slipped off her top to reveal a baby-blue bustier.

He should stop her, but as she stepped from her skirt and turned toward him in her garter and stockings all he could manage was an unenthusiastic, "Wait."

"I was dying for you to see me in this." She crooked her finger and, like a puppet, he moved on wooden legs to stand before her.

Even as disillusionment and desire warred in him, he let his hands skim over her hips. "You don't have to play the sexy siren with me, Crystal."

"But I want to, Sam. I want to show you all you've taught me. We can play with your camera again. I'll pose for you. I'll be your own calendar girl."

The air around her shimmered with sensuality. She *was* every bit the calendar model. But in that moment he longed for the old Crystal.

With a monumental effort, he stepped away from her. "I'm no photographer. Not a single picture I took turned out. Guess I was too distracted."

"That's okay. I'm not really interested in the pictures." She stepped closer to him, but he held her off.

"Let's head out to the ball field, practice some passes," he said.

Her forehead furrowed in confusion, then she laughed. "Yeah, right, like I could catch a pass in these shoes."

"You could take them off."

"I'd ruin my clothes."

"They're just clothes."

She cocked her head and gave him a sultry smile. "But are you so sure you want me to get dressed? Don't you like my new outfit?"

"I'd have to be dead not to appreciate you in that, but haven't you gotten what you wanted? You'll make the calendar cut. You'll win the guy. You don't need me anymore. Look at you."

He let his gaze sweep over her. "You've reached the top, sweetheart. You're all you set out to be and more. There isn't a woman around who can hold a candle to you." His throat constricted. "My job is done."

Her eyes widened. "Oh, but I do need you."

"No, Crystal. You don't.

"I think I know what I want."

"You said you wanted Kincaid."

"I was wrong about that."

"So what makes you so sure that you know what you want now?"

She raised her chin and attempted a smile, though the corners fell just short of lifting. "This is the new me. I know what I want now."

She moved to close the gap between them, but he held her at arm's length. "I liked the old you."

"Yeah." She laughed a harsh little laugh. "You liked me as one of the guys."

"Let me tell you what I liked about the old Crystal."

She frowned and started to move away, but he took her hands and held them fast. He waited until she stilled and looked at him, then he continued, "I liked the way you never worried about what other people thought of you. I liked how pleasing yourself was always enough.''

''I don't know, sounds a little selfish. Maybe I've grown beyond that.''

''I liked the way you went after everything with gusto, how you never pulled any punches. I liked how you laughed that full-bellied, snorting kind of laugh and how you always put your friends and family first over everything else.''

She shook her head and tried to pull away, but he held her fast. He cocked his head, willing her to listen, really listen to him. ''I loved how you put your heart and soul into everything you did, from your latest article on bathroom decor to the relationships with those of us who were fortunate enough to be a part of your life.''

He drew a breath as she raised her gaze to his and he continued, ''I loved how you took the bull by the horns and accomplished any goal you took on.''

''You're wrong about me, Sam.'' Disappointment and sadness filled her eyes, weighed down her voice, making her sound lost and so vulnerable. ''I'm not that girl. I never was.''

He opened his mouth to respond, but she stopped him with a finger to his lips. Her gaze dropped to his mouth for a moment, before drifting back up to his eyes. ''I'm so sorry. I wouldn't know where to begin to become that girl. I just don't think I have it in me.''

She turned, then ran from the room before he could utter a sound to stop her.

WIND WHIPPED THROUGH the treetops surrounding Crystal's apartment, lashing them with a ferocity that matched her mood. She slammed her bedroom door, then stripped off her clothes. Tears swelled in her eyes as she fumbled over the zipper on the bustier. When it gave way, she tore off the garment, then the garter and stockings.

Fuming, she slipped on her oldest T-shirt and a pair of sweats. How could she have been so wrong about Sam? Every bone in her body told her he cared for her on a level much deeper than he'd ever verbalized. Yet, he'd rejected her earlier overture.

Humiliation burned in her cheeks. She'd stood there before him, dressed for seduction, and he'd barely blinked an eye. What did it mean? Had he *really* wanted to head out to the park?

I liked how you laughed that full-bellied, snorting kind of laugh and how you always put your friends and family first over everything else.

Put her friends and family first? She sank to her bed and let the misery overtake her. She'd let them all down: Cami, her mother, her father, even Megs might never speak to her again. Crystal might have broken the record for alienating the most loved ones in a single day.

Sure, Megs had said some hateful things, but what had she said that wasn't true? Besides, she'd been distraught over how badly things had gone with Leo. Crystal *had* told her to call off the wedding.

Somehow she had to find a way to make it up to everyone.

And the worst of it was that she had no idea how to fix things. She was writing this article on family reunions and her own family seemed to be falling apart. *Blending the old with the new.* Was there a way to use that theme to patch up her family's troubles?

She lay for a moment, staring at the ceiling, thoughts swirling through her mind. Maybe there was a way, but first she had a deadline and it was high time she finished this article. Drawing a fortifying breath, she rolled from the bed, then headed for her computer.

"CRYSTAL?"

Crystal's heart quickened at the sound of the male voice on her phone. Then her mind registered that it wasn't Sam and disappointment flooded her. "Yes?"

"Hi, this is Ron Kincaid."

"Hello, Ron. How are you?"

"I'm great. And you?"

"I'm great, too."

His soft chuckle sent a measure of warmth flowing through her. Maybe he didn't instill the same kind of heart-throbbing, breath-stealing, knee-weakening reaction in her that Sam did, but still he was a nice guy—nicer than too many people gave him credit for.

Why was he calling?

"I missed you at the park today."

"The park?" She glanced at her calendar. Was it Saturday? She'd been in a haze for the past few days.

"Yeah, I think your team missed you, too. They didn't do very well. Course with Schaffer out, too, they were bound to get creamed."

"Sam wasn't there?"

"No, I guess I'm glad you didn't know. I wondered if the two of you were off together somewhere."

"Oh..." Her throat tightened. "There's nothing going on with me and Sam."

Not anymore. Not after the other night.

"Great. I wasn't sure, you know, after the gallery. Listen, this is kind of last minute, but I was hoping I could interest you in dinner tonight, since you were busy last time I asked."

"Dinner?" She'd been trying to reach her family and Cami for the past few days. No one seemed available, at least to her.

She'd somehow gotten the reunion article in just under the wire. Since Sam's rejection she'd thrown herself into the makeover series. She'd written almost nonstop, outlining the three articles, then finishing the rough draft of the first one.

Dinner? Why not? It wasn't as if anyone else was beating down her door to spend time with her.

"Sure. Dinner would be nice." She checked her clock. It was nearly five already. "What time?"

"Seven-thirty?"

She ran her hand through her disheveled hair and clutched her robe around her. Could she transform herself in time? "Sure, seven-thirty's fine."

"That's great. What's your address?"

After giving him her address, she disconnected, then dropped the phone and groaned. Thoughts of Sam drifted through her mind and an overwhelming sense of loss filled her. Should she call him?

No, she was a big girl and she could get herself ready. Besides, he'd made it pretty clear he felt his job as her mentor was over. Still, a little part of her ached to hear his voice again. If she told him she had accepted Ron's invitation, was there a chance Sam might be the tiniest bit jealous?

Groaning at her own weakness, she turned away from the phone. Hadn't she humiliated herself enough the other night? With a sigh, she headed for the shower. She hadn't gone two steps when the ringing of the phone summoned her back.

She stared at it a moment as it rang again. Who could it be? Cami? Her mother or father or Megs? She'd certainly left enough messages for each of them. As she reached for the receiver the most stubborn part of her that refused to let the dream die, hoped it was Sam.

"Hello?" Her heart thrummed in her throat.

"Hey." The one simple syllable voiced in that sexy baritone sent excited shivers up her spine.

"Sam." She stood, clutching the phone and feeling like a schoolgirl dying to be asked to the prom.

"I hear we got creamed today."

"Yeah, I heard the same. I missed it, too."

"I just wanted to check on you—make sure you're all right. You were upset over your family and Cami the other night and I didn't really get a chance to see if there was anything I could do to help. You kind of distracted me."

Heat bloomed in her cheeks. She'd distracted him so much in her little outfit he'd wanted her to get dressed to go play ball.

"That's okay. I'm kind of in limbo with all of them. I've left messages for everyone, but no one's called me back. Guess they're all mad at me."

"Well, that's their loss."

He was silent a moment and she bit the inside of

her cheek, not knowing what to say, but desperate to keep him on the phone.

"Crystal?"

"Yes?"

"I'm sorry…about the other night."

Relief washed over her. Maybe they could salvage something of their relationship. "Me, too. It was so silly of me to run off like that. So, you wanted to play ball. It wasn't quite what I had hoped we do, but—"

"I wish I could make you understand."

"It's okay. Remember, no strings. If you're done mentoring me, then you're done." Her throat burned and she cursed the tears swimming in her eyes.

Why the hell had she thought she could sleep with him and not get emotionally attached?

"I'm glad you understand."

She nodded, her throat burning, then she realized he couldn't see her. She swallowed. "Sure. No hard feelings. We're still friends, right?"

He hesitated a long moment and she swiped at the tears spilling down her cheeks. He said, "As long as you want me."

I want you. "Great. Hey, you'll never guess who just called."

"Ron. He asked you out."

"You are a spoilsport. You're supposed to let me tell you." She drew a shaky breath and resisted the urge to beg him to come over.

"He's taking you to Nava tonight."

"Well, probably. He's taking me to dinner. He didn't say where. He'll be here at seven-thirty."

"Wear the red dress."

Her heart dropped. She'd been saving the red dress

for him. Of course, that was no longer appropriate. "You sure? I thought you said I should save that one."

"It wasn't right for a first impression, but for tonight, it's perfect."

"How can you be so sure?"

"Instinct. Isn't that why you asked for my help in the first place?"

"Well, yes, but—"

"Then don't question it, unless you no longer need my advice, now that I'm not...mentoring you."

"No, that's great. I'd love your advice." Did he hear the little catch in her voice?

"Wear the red."

"The red it is."

"Wear your hair up."

"Up?"

"Yes, the way you had it that first day."

"Do I have to roll it?"

"I'll send Loni."

"No, Sam, I don't need Loni."

"Very well...will you be able to manage?"

No. "Yes, I'll muddle through it. You've been a wonderful help to me, Sam." She bit her lip and let the tears roll freely. "Thank you."

"Crystal—"

"I'd better go hop in the shower."

"Right. Call me if you need me."

"Okay."

Silence buzzed across the line, then Sam spoke. "Knock him dead, sweetheart. He'll ask you to do a shoot for the calendar. Maybe not tonight, but soon."

"You think so?"

"He doesn't make hasty decisions where his work is concerned. He'll take his time to mull things over, so don't get discouraged."

Discouraged? She was on her way to hard-core depression. "Right."

"I'll talk to you soon."

"Sam."

Another pause, then, "Yes?"

"I'm really glad you called."

"Me, too. I need to go. I've got some papers I need to go over."

"Right, okay, well, don't work too hard. You can't go from playboy to workaholic in one night."

He chuckled softly and the sound warmed her. "No trouble there. I'm hanging up now. Go get ready."

"Goodbye."

The phone clicked in her ear. She hung up, then stood for a moment with her hand on the receiver. Then she wiped away the last of her tears and headed for the shower.

13

"COULD YOU EXCUSE ME, RON? I need to run to the ladies' room." Crystal smiled at the photographer as she pushed back from the table. If she couldn't get away for a few minutes, where she could relax and wipe this fake smile off her face, she might go mad.

"You bet, love. Just hurry back."

She threaded her way through the same tables she'd maneuvered around a short while ago. Had it really been almost three weeks? It seemed a lifetime had come and gone.

"Crystal."

She jerked up her head. Cami waved from the bar. "Cami?"

Any trepidation she might have felt over seeing her friend evaporated as Cami rushed toward her, her arms outstretched and Crystal found herself wrapped in her embrace. Cami drew back and said, "I'm so glad I ran into you. I'm so sorry. Are you mad at me?"

"Me, mad at *you*?" Crystal stared at her in confusion. "I can't believe you're even talking to me. Why on earth would I be mad at you?"

Cami shook her head. "I got so wrapped up in everything, I never checked messages until about half an hour ago."

"So what are you doing here? What's going on with Parker?"

"Parker's at home. I came to get our takeout."

"So, you and he..."

She hesitated a long moment. "We're working things out. I'm so sorry I didn't call you back."

"My God, Cami, I've been so worried. All hell broke loose this week. Where have you been?"

"Well, Parker took off—that's when I left you that message—he was so upset. I called around and found him at his brother's in Dawsonville. He wouldn't talk to me, so I jumped in my car and headed up there. I took off some vacation time. We've been talking for days." She shrugged. "At least I got him to come back with me. I'm not sure where we'll go from here."

"I looked everywhere for you. I wanted to make sure you were okay."

Cami's cheeks flushed. "I think I knew he wasn't planning on coming back and I sort of freaked out. It wasn't pretty."

Crystal hugged her. "I'm so sorry. But you think you'll be okay? You're working everything out?"

"I honestly don't know. Things are strained, but I'm doing everything I can to make it up to him." She drew a shaky breath. "So, look at you in that red dress. Honey, you are turning some heads tonight."

"Well, Sam suggested the dress."

"Is he here?" Cami glanced around the restaurant.

"No, I'm here with Ron."

"Oh." Her eyebrows drew together. "How's that going?"

''Fine. You know, he's a really great guy. He's smart. He's talented. He's gorgeous—''

''But he's not Sam.''

''Sam and I are over.'' Crystal shrugged and willed her voice to stay steady. ''We're still friends, though.''

''And he suggested you wear the red dress for Ron?''

''He called right after Ron. He's still willing to give me advice, which heaven knows I can use.''

Cami cocked her head. ''Are you sure you're okay? You don't seem too thrilled.''

''Oh, yeah, just had a rough week with my folks. My dad quit his job and my mother is fuming over it. Oh, and Megs ended things with Leo and blames me for leading her astray.''

''Oh, honey…'' Cami gave her a big hug. ''And on top of it all, you and Sam broke it off. You did have a rough week. I'm so sorry I wasn't here for you.''

''We didn't break anything off. There was never anything to break off.'' She closed her eyes and swallowed. ''I went to see him the other night, all dressed up to seduce him and he said I didn't need his mentoring anymore.''

''Just like that?''

A choked laugh escaped her. ''He said he wanted to head out to the ball field, toss a few balls. There I was in this bustier and G-string and he wanted to exercise his throwing arm.''

''Honey, maybe he just missed the old you.''

''That's exactly what he said. Except the old me he remembers never existed.''

"You sure? I thought the old you was pretty awesome, just like the new you, only with more comfy clothes."

"It's not funny."

"No, I'm not saying it is, but you want to know something? Parker said the same thing to me."

"He did? But he's the one who bought you that gift certificate for your makeover."

"I'm not saying he didn't like the new me. Well, not the new me that couldn't control the flirting or that kissed the guy at work, but he liked the new me that had eyes only for him. When we were alone, he loved to have me get all gorgeous just for him.

"But he said he missed the old me, too. I thought about your article, with the old and the new and we talked about a compromise. I'm hopeful it will work. At least he's willing to give it a shot."

"What kind of compromise?"

"I can be the new me whenever I feel like it, as long as I control the flirting and when he misses the old me, he just says so and I'm back in my cotton undies in a flash."

"But you're not sure it will work?"

"He's still upset with me. That man has a temper."

"Well, I'm betting you work it out."

"I hope so. Hey, if there's hope for us, there's hope for you…and Sam."

"I told you, there is no me and Sam to work out. He's not interested. He made that very clear."

"Don't you see? That night he wasn't rejecting you. He was just missing the old you."

"So, I should have sucked it up and played ball?"

"Maybe. It's worth a try, though, don't you think? If you want there to be a you and Sam, that is."

Crystal frowned. "But the old me was just one of the guys to him. He was never interested in the old me in that way."

"That's where you blend the old with the new."

"I dress like the old me, but I bring along my new attitude?" Doubt plagued her.

"That's it. If you really want it. It's worth a try, isn't it?"

"I don't know, Cami. It really hurt to be rejected like that. I don't know if I could survive another round."

Cami's eyes darkened and she frowned. "Just promise me you'll think about it, okay?"

"Sure." Crystal forced a smile. "I'll give it some thought."

CRYSTAL STARED AT THE BLANK screen—the blinking cursor—and murmured to herself. Focus, Peterson.

"If I were an *Edge* subscriber, what would I want to read about? Sex, women, cars, sports, having sex with women in cars and during sporting events or having sex as a sporting event. Or just playing sports, then having sex, probably in that order. No."

She closed her eyes, blotting out the damned cursor that seemed to blink her lack of real talent into existence. She could beat this round of writer's block. She could beat the damn cursor.

Still, thoughts of Sam intruded as they had since she'd last seen him. She couldn't get the memory of his look of disappointment out of her head. Even on opening her eyes, his disappointment seemed to frown down on her, like some specter that had settled over her. "What do you want?" she asked the ghost—Sam's ghost, the ghost of what she could have had, if she'd only been the girl of his imagination.

The cursor blinked. She let loose a vicious snarl. "I can't do this. I can't write this column. I don't have the talent. I can't even come up with one lousy idea."

Silence weighed down on her. She frowned at the screen. Maybe if she just started writing something—anything—an idea would come. She placed her fingers on the keyboard and started typing.

We've all had the experience of chasing rainbows, looking for those elusive pots of gold. Maybe not real rainbows and real gold, but something that shimmers and calls to us much the same way.

I have recently had this experience and I was fortunate, or unfortunate, enough to find my pot of gold. How can finding the gold be unfortunate? Well, I've learned the hard way the painful truth of that age-old saying that all that glitters is not gold.

Once the words began to flow, she relaxed and let them slide off her fingertips onto the keyboard. At one point during the night, she glanced at the cursor as it blinked at the start of a fresh page…and smiled.

HOW COULD HE HAVE TURNED Crystal away? The scene rolled again through Sam's mind the following Friday, as it had countless times over the past week. Each time he fantasized a different outcome, one where he accepted her as she was and took what she'd come to offer.

And each time left him feeling empty, because all

she offered was the new outer self she'd discovered through her makeover. It just wasn't enough. He wanted all of her. He wanted the real Crystal he'd come to know over the years.

God, he missed her.

Tammy, his administrative assistant, knocked on his door. He called for her to enter, then quickly signed the stack of papers she held in front of him. They went over some important items on his calendar, then he could bear no more. He wanted to be alone in his misery.

''That's it, Tammy. Could you pull the door to behind you?'' Sam clutched his pen while his assistant gathered up her notepad, then quietly left.

He dropped his head into his hands, resisting the urge to call Crystal and see how she was doing. She'd called him enough over the past week, while Kincaid took her to Nava or the High or to that art gallery where he sometimes did showings of his photography.

The buzzer on Sam's intercom startled him from his reverie.

''Sam?'' Tammy's voice sounded over the phone's speaker.

''Yes?''

''Ron Kincaid is here to see you.''

Kincaid? He was the last person Sam wanted to see.

''He says he doesn't have an appointment, but you asked him to stop by.''

''Right, show him in.'' Hell, during dinner that first night at Nava, when Kincaid had let his real character show through with Sheila, Sam had actually felt sorry for him and told him to stop by to discuss some upcoming projects.

When Tammy showed him in, Sam half rose to shake his hand, then motioned to one of the chairs near his desk.

"Did I catch you at a good time?" Kincaid asked. "I meant to drop by last week, but got sidetracked with a few things. I was actually in the building today, so this works out, if you've got a minute."

"Sure, now's fine." Sam steepled his fingers. Maybe they could tie this up pretty quickly. "I've got a couple of projects my regular photographer might not be able to get to as soon as I'd like."

Kincaid flipped open his handheld, then scrolled through his calendar. "I have a couple of days open over the next few weeks, then I'm out for about a week while we do the calendar shoot in Florida. I'll have more time after that, though."

"I need someone to head to the Keys for a day or two to shoot an old bar there purported to have the loveliest waitresses in the northern hemisphere."

"Your guy's passing that up?"

"He's not too keen on the Keys. Had a run-in with a shark off the coast once. I've had trouble getting him to go back ever since."

"Poor sap. Okay, I think I can handle that."

They settled on the dates and other details, then discussed one other project, before they sealed the whole deal with a handshake.

"I'll have Tammy forward you the standard paperwork."

"That's great. Thanks." Kincaid shifted in his seat.

"So, can I ask you something of a more personal nature?"

Sam tensed. "I suppose so. What can I help you with?"

Kincaid stretched his neck and for the first time that Sam could remember, the guy appeared unsure of himself. "So, how's Crystal? I mean, you two are friends and all and I thought you might have spoken to her lately."

"I think you've seen a little more of her these past days than I have."

"Well, we have been seeing a good bit of each other." His face fell and no man had ever looked more confused. "She's a really great girl. She's beautiful, she's charming. She can talk sports just like any guy and she's so damn hot. All I can think about is jumping her, but I've held back all week." He laughed. "That's a new one for me."

Sam let out his breath and relaxed a fraction. "Some women are worth getting to know first."

"Exactly. It's the strangest experience. I think we're actually at the start of something here. I mean, this could be the real thing."

"And you think I'd be interested in this because..."

"I don't know. You're friends with her. I thought maybe she's said something, given you some insight into how she feels about the whole thing."

"Like I said, we haven't had much opportunity to talk lately."

Kincaid sat silent for a moment, considering. "I've got the photos from her shoot." He motioned to his briefcase. "I'm going to take them to her to show her. I'm going to tell her I want her for the calendar."

Sam nodded, all his muscles tensing. "She should be thrilled."

"You think so? And I'm going to ask her to go away with me this weekend. What do you think? I don't want to pressure her into anything before she's ready."

Sam's heart thudded dully. He'd lost. This was it. Crystal had gotten all she'd set out for. She'd gotten the calendar spot and she'd gotten the guy. Game over.

"Let me see them." He fixed his gaze on Ron's briefcase.

"Her pictures from the test shoot?"

"Yeah."

"They're amazing." He pulled a large envelope from his bag. "Here." He spread the half-dozen photographs over Sam's desk. "She's a natural. Funny, all these months, with this feminine powerhouse right under my nose. She's the most sensual woman I've ever met. How did I miss it?"

Sam's gaze swept the pictures and his gut tightened. He stared speechless, fighting the urge to sweep up the telling photos and lock them away where no other man could gaze on her passion-filled eyes, her curves ripe for touching.

His throat tightened. A light shone in her eyes. It spoke volumes. It spoke of joy and deep emotion… maybe even love.

And she'd done this for Kincaid and his camera. There she'd been, half naked and alone with the man. Had she thought of the photographer touching her, tasting her? What fantasies had she dreamed up of the two of them to put that heat—that light—in her eyes?

Kincaid cleared his throat beside him. ''Well?''

Sam straightened and pulled his gaze from the images. A sick feeling spread through him. ''I'd say she's ready for that weekend.''

A wide smile spread across Kincaid's face. ''Great. I'm going to see her now.'' He scooped up the photographs, then slid them back into the envelope.

He straightened and extended his hand to Sam. ''Thanks, for everything.''

Sam gripped his hand and met Kincaid's gaze with a stern stare. ''She's really special and I have to tell you that if you don't treat her right, I'll beat the hell out of you.''

Kincaid's head snapped up and his eyes widened in surprise. ''Shit. If I didn't know better, I'd say you're in love with her.''

Sam let go of Kincaid's hand. ''Just treat her right.''

Kincaid's eyebrows knit. ''I will, buddy.''

With that, he turned, then left, leaving Sam with the tortured memory of Crystal's photographs.

CRYSTAL'S PHONE SUMMONED her from her computer. Blowing out a breath, she tore her gaze from the screen. ''Hello?''

''Hello, sunshine.''

''Ron. Hi, how are you?''

''Wonderful, now that I hear your voice. I know you're probably busy right now with your writing, but I was hoping I could stop by for a few minutes.''

''Actually, I'm taking a break right now, so it

would be a good time,'' she lied, guilt over writing the article for Sam filling her.

She shook it off. So she was dating one man and pining for another. She'd made a deal with Sam to try her hand at the column. She had no reason to feel guilty over fulfilling her business obligations. It was the personal fantasies she had while writing the article that heated her cheeks.

''I was hoping you'd say that. I'm pulling into your complex.''

''Great.'' She forced some enthusiasm into her voice, irrationally annoyed with him. He was taking time out of his day to drop by to see her. This was good…wasn't it?

She stepped out onto her front porch. He smiled brightly and waved as he exited his car, briefcase in hand. He bounded up her stairs, two at a time, then swept her into his arms and spun her around, before setting her on her feet again.

Sadly, her heart no longer raced at the sight of him, at his touch. Why couldn't he make her feel the way Sam made her feel?

''I'm so glad you were home and able to see me.''

''Well, I have a few minutes, then I need to get back to work.''

''Right, your deadline.'' He took her hand and pulled her toward the door. ''Let's go inside. I want to show you something.''

Her gaze flickered over the briefcase in his hand and her heart did quicken. Could he have brought the pictures from her trial shoot? He wasted no time in guiding her to the light-filled sunroom.

''Here, sit here, get comfortable. I promise this

won't take long.'' He settled her onto the rattan love seat, then kneeled beside the wicker chest that doubled as a coffee table. With precise movements, he spread out about half a dozen photographs over the magazines covering the surface.

A roaring sounded in Crystal's ears as she gazed, stunned, at the images. Heat climbed up her neck and pricked her scalp. She lifted one of the pictures, almost hesitant to touch it. ''Is this me?''

''Do you like them?'' Ron pinned her with a steady gaze.

''I...don't know what to say. I look so...so...''

''Sensual.''

''So...loose.''

''Not at all. Sweetheart, out of all the calendar candidates I've shot over the past weeks, these are by far the hottest, most genuine—you have an earthiness that just comes across for the camera. It can't be affected, or copied. This—'' he gestured with a sweeping motion ''—comes from inside.''

He turned to her and his gaze burned brighter, the way it had that afternoon of the shoot. ''You're a natural. I want you for the calendar.''

''Oh.'' The muscles in her stomach tightened and her whole body seemed to go boneless.

''We travel to the Florida Panhandle in about a week. We're still finalizing the details.''

She nodded.

''So, what do you say?''

She stared at the pictures, the tension in her stomach turning into a real ache. She felt raw, exposed. Who was that woman in the pictures?''

''I want to feature you on the cover, as well as

inside the calendar. There won't be a man out there who'll be able to resist. These babies'll sell like hot-cakes. Hell, even the women will go nuts. They'll all be beating a line for Secret Temptations, wanting to create the same look."

He brushed his fingers across her cheeks. "None of them will come close, though. You're awesome, Crystal. Come away with me. I want to take you to Saint Simons for the weekend. I've got a condo on the beach there."

Blood roared in her ears. She didn't want this. She didn't want to be eye candy for the drooling male masses. And how could she ever go away with Ron for an entire weekend, when she couldn't go half an hour without thinking of Sam?

"Ron, I'm…overwhelmed—"

"I know, it's a lot to take in. Listen, why don't you take some time to think about it. I don't need an answer right now. Take a couple of days—"

"I don't need a couple of days." She leaned forward and collected the pictures into a neat stack. When she'd finished, she slipped them back into the envelope.

Regret flooded her. Why couldn't she fall back in love with Ron and forget about Sam? Life would be so much easier then. Here she'd spent all this time and energy to capture Ron's interest and she'd succeeded beyond her wildest dreams. She'd gotten exactly what she'd asked for—and found she didn't want it.

She squared her shoulders and faced him. "I can't do this. Not the calendar and, I'm so sorry, but I can't go away for the weekend with you."

He nodded slowly, his expression grim. "You can't or you won't?"

"Both. I can't do what isn't in my heart to do."

He stared at her a long moment. A roughness colored his voice when he spoke, "It really hurts to hear that, both professionally and personally, but I'm glad you're shooting straight with me."

"Thanks for understanding."

"My guess is that there's someone else you're not shooting it straight with."

Her eyebrows rounded in surprise. "I'm not so sure everyone else in the world is so ready to hear the truth."

"You don't think so?" A knowing smile curved his lips and his eyes sparkled. He really was such a good-looking man. It was a complete shame that he just didn't do it for her anymore. "Maybe you should give it a try. What have you got to lose?"

"Thanks, I'll think about it."

She stared after him, long after he'd gone. One thought circled in her mind. What *did* she have to lose?

"SAM." HIS FATHER DREW BACK, surprise arching his eyebrows. He looked rested and more at ease than Sam had seen him in a long time. "Come in. Come in. It's great to see you." He gestured for Sam to enter.

Sam stepped inside his father's penthouse home. Designer furniture filled the apartment's open spaces. Limited edition prints covered the walls. His father certainly didn't lack in material comforts. "Hope I'm not intruding."

''No, son, not at all. Can I get you anything? A beer?''

''I'm good, thanks.''

''Well, come out here with me and sit down.'' He led Sam out onto his twentieth-floor balcony. Atlanta's midtown skyline stretched before them. A grill at one end of the patio gave off the tempting aroma of cooking meat.

''Sit.'' His father waved Sam toward a cushioned chair as he turned to the grill. ''I'm cooking a little steak for my dinner. Want some?''

''No. I'm not staying.''

''I'm glad you stopped by.'' He flipped his steak, then settled into a chair beside Sam. ''I called you twice this past week, but you were on the phone or in meetings. I didn't leave a message.''

''I'm surprised Tammy didn't recognize you and put you through.''

''It doesn't matter.'' He shifted. ''I needed to say this in person. I was going to call you tomorrow, see if we could get together. Didn't expect to find you at my door on a Friday night. You should be out with some sweet young thing.''

Sam waved his comment aside. ''I stopped by to talk to you about the board meeting.''

His father held up his hand. ''Maggie tells me I'm an old coot. I've decided she's right.''

''Who's Maggie?''

''Ah, there's a gem. I went to this healing expo about a month ago, over by the Waverly. Don't know exactly why. I was over there for something else.'' He frowned. ''Doesn't matter. I saw the signs. There was a workshop starting on healing alternatives for cancer, so I walked on in, decided to see what it was all about.''

''Dad—''

''And there she was. What an angel. She looked up and smiled, patted the seat beside her and I plopped myself down there. I have no idea what that seminar was about, but I thank the Almighty every day for leading me to her.''

''So, you're dating this woman?''

He shook his head. ''I don't know what she sees in me.''

''You need to be careful.''

''Ah, I know, she could be after my money, but I don't think so. Don't care if she is.'' He leaned in closer to Sam. ''She's got a healing touch, I tell you. I've slowly started feeling better since I met her. Seems like recently we've been seeing more of each other and just being with her does wonders for me. I can be feeling so wrung out, then Maggie touches me and…ah, well, I feel like I could go out and conquer the world. I haven't felt this good in years.''

''I'm glad you've found someone, Dad. I really hope it works out.''

''Oh, it already has. That's the beauty of it. I cherish each day I have with her, but if she were to leave tomorrow, I'd know she's already given me a lifetime worth of loving.''

A memory of his father, downtrodden and depressed flashed through Sam's mind. ''And you'd just let her go? You'd be okay with that?''

''Sure. I know what you're thinking. I took it hard when your mother left me. It took me years to realize that was her failure, not mine.''

"But you put so much into that marriage." The old resentment rose in him.

"And I don't regret a minute of it. If I had my life to do over again, I wouldn't change a thing." Color stained his cheeks. "Except maybe that board meeting."

"About the board meeting—"

"Maggie's helped me to see that I've got a few control issues."

"Only a few?" Sam quirked his eyebrow.

His father chuckled. "Okay, maybe more than a few. The point is that I'm willing to concede that I may have been a little rigid at that meeting."

"Change is good, but not if it's going to cause strife. I don't want to move forward without your support. I respect that you have years of experience at this."

"Well, I appreciate that. I can't promise that I'll be able to turn a new leaf overnight. I'm still hesitant about all this change, but like I said before, new blood is a good thing. I'm willing to give a little in that respect."

Sam grinned. "How much is a little?"

"Can we play that one by ear? With the understanding that I'll do my best to be a little more open-minded?"

"Sure. I'm sure we'll butt heads some more as we go along. I don't suppose we'll always see eye to eye about how to run the magazine."

"We'll be okay if we keep in mind we both have something to bring to the table."

"I'd like to meet this Maggie. She sounds like one smart lady."

''I'm thinking about traveling to Europe this fall, asking her to go with me.''

''Well, like I said, I hope it all works out.''

''Oh, it will, son. You can bet on it.''

As Sam bid his father farewell, a sense of contentment filled him. Maybe they weren't resolving all their issues here, but this was a start.

14

PAIGE STEELS SMILED at Sam as he stood in her open door. ''Hello, Sam. Come on in. We were just watching some TV.''

The TV glowed softly from its place in the floor-to-ceiling entertainment center. The peppy tunes of a commercial played as some actor hawked muscle cream. Steels turned from his spot on the sofa. ''Hey, bro. What's up?''

''Not much. Thought I'd come help you move furniture out of that back room like I promised.''

''That would be great. Gotta make room for the new addition. Take a load off first, though. What's doing?''

Sam dropped into an armchair set at an angle to the sofa. Paige settled by her husband, snuggling easily into his side. Steels had met her when she'd moved to Atlanta shortly after that fated camping trip. In one way or another, they'd been together ever since. High-school combatants turned college sweethearts. Who'd have thought they'd last? Yet here they were, expecting their second child.

''So, how's your father doing?'' she asked.

''He's good. I just left him, actually. He looks better than he has in a long while, even though he's seemed a little beat recently. He was feisty enough during the last board meeting, though.'' Sam shook his head. ''He can be the most aggravating man and I worry about him, but he's a survivor.''

Steels nodded. ''Give him our best the next time you see him.''

''Sure.'' Sam drew a deep breath as another commercial flickered across the screen. ''He really wants us to win that award.''

''Think you will?'' Steels asked.

A child's cry sounded from one of the back bedrooms and Paige excused herself to see to their daughter, giving Steels a quick kiss on his cheek before she pulled away. Something about the gesture and the loving look in her eyes tightened Sam's chest.

''Probably not this year,'' Sam answered once she'd gone. ''But I think we'd have a good shot next year, if I could get Crystal to take on that new column.''

''She's not interested?''

''I think she's a little intimidated by it. But I know she could do it, if she'd just trust herself.''

''Maybe all she needs is a little encouragement.''

Encouragement. Would she be more inclined to take on the column now that she'd built up her confidence by winning Kincaid? ''We've worked out a deal. She's going to give it a shot.''

''That's what all that makeover stuff was about.'' Steels shrugged. ''Paige heard about it from one of the girls, who heard from Megs or someone.''

Sam nodded. ''Word does get around.''

''But I thought she said she wasn't interested in a makeover.''

''She got it into her head that she wanted to be eye candy for Kincaid's calendar.''

Steels's eyebrows arched. ''Crystal wants to be one of his calendar hotties?''

''She thinks it'll help him notice her.''

''Oh.'' Understanding lit Steels's gray eyes. ''She's got the hots for Kincaid.''

''Apparently.'' Sam kept his tone neutral. ''At least she did for a while. I don't know. I'm not sure what's going on with her anymore. Seems they've been seeing a lot of each other lately.''

''And you don't approve? Of her and our photographer friend.''

''She deserves better.''

''Kincaid's okay. He gets more than his share of women, but that's understandable in his line of work. I could say the same thing about you. Must be nice being the youngest CEO in *Edge* history.''

Sam frowned. Was he so much like Kincaid?

An unwanted vision of Crystal posing for Kincaid flashed through Sam's mind. He shrugged, trying to dislodge the tightness in his chest that settled in whenever he thought of her with the photographer. ''They did a trial shoot Tuesday before last.''

''For the calendar? So she's really going to be in it?''

The memory of her in the bustier and G-string burned through his mind. ''That's my understanding. Kincaid was supposed to ask her today. Surprises me he took so long. The guy takes his time making decisions.''

''You spoke with her?''

''Crystal? I've spoken with her on and off, though

I haven't seen her since she stopped by after the shoot.''

''After the shoot with Kincaid? She came to see you?''

''It was late that evening and just briefly.'' Then he'd upset her and sent her running. *Idiot.*

''You're kidding.''

''No. Why?''

''Crystal did a shoot with Kincaid, dressed in some skimpy kind of lingerie, then she showed up at your place afterward?''

Irritation grated through Sam. ''I believe that's what I said.''

''Don't you see?''

Sam stared at him.

''That doesn't jive with Kincaid's MO.''

''So?''

''He always dates his models. Think about it. Now, I can only imagine that Crystal was one major hottie in whatever she was wearing. He's going to spend a couple hours with that and not ask her out to dinner? You know, that's his MO, then after dinner he always gets the payoff.''

Sam bristled. ''Well, maybe she wasn't interested in the payoff. In fact, from what he says, they've gone out all week and there still hasn't been a payoff.''

''Bingo. Paige, bring the man a beer. He gets the prize or, in this case, I'm guessing the girl.''

To Sam's surprise, Paige strode into the room, bearing two bottles of beer and a tired smile. She handed each man a beer, then settled beside her husband.

She turned to Sam. ''Hallelujah. I didn't think you

two would ever work things out. So, what are you doing *here?* I mean, I'm dying to get started on the baby's room, but it can wait another day or two."

Sam frowned first at Paige, then Steels. "Did I miss something?"

Steels shifted uncomfortably. "Now, honey, maybe we shouldn't butt in."

"Butt in?" She regarded him with raised eyebrows. "Is that what caring for your friends is called?"

"I'm just saying, if Sam wants our help, he'll let us know."

"He's here, isn't he?"

Steels set down his beer and turned to Sam. "She has a point."

"I'm here to help move furniture."

"Sam Schaffer." Paige pierced him with a stare reminiscent of any grade-school teacher's. "Are you telling me that you passed up an evening with a fine woman like Crystal, that you've let her run all over town this week with that photographer, and that now you want to spend your Friday night helping us married folk clear out that room?"

He blinked at her. Maybe he did need help.

"Man, you didn't actually, like, ask her to leave that night after the shoot?" Steels stared at him as if he'd lost his mind.

Maybe he had.

"No, she got upset and ran off. I didn't ask her to leave. I just wanted to head out to the ball field."

"And that upset her?" Steels scratched his head. "Crystal loves to play ball."

A disgruntled sound came from Paige's direction.

''Maybe she doesn't want to play ball all the time. Maybe sometimes she'd like to pursue *other* interests.''

Light seemed to break over Steels's face. ''Come on, Schaffer, she didn't want to...and you didn't...''

Sam gritted his teeth. A vision of the blue of Crystal's bustier reflected in the blue of her eyes swam before him. He sat silent and stiff.

Steels stood and clapped his hands together. ''Okay, I'm game if the man wants to move furniture.''

''Actually, bro, I think I'd like to take a rain check.'' Sam rose and faced his friend.

A smile lit Paige's face and Steels grinned as he shook his head. ''Do you know what kind of trouble you're in for?''

Sam's gaze traveled from husband to wife. The fights these two had had. ''Is it worth it?''

''You bet.'' Steels scooped Paige to his side and kissed her cheek. ''Wouldn't have it any other way.''

''He's still a pain at times, but overall he'll do.'' Her radiant smile took any sting out of her words.

Could Sam let out his feelings for Crystal? His father certainly wasn't holding back anything for this Maggie woman. He, of all people, would have reason to clamp down on his emotions. Still, Sam had cloistered away his feelings for so long, was it even possible to let them go now?

Actually, I've had second thoughts about Ron.

Exactly what had she meant by that? Had she really given up on the photographer—lost interest that easily—then run back to him, when Sam had ruined her plans for seduction?

"Thanks for the beer...and the company," he said.

He turned to leave, but Paige called to him, saying, "If she wanted Ron, what was she doing at your place that night?"

"I don't know and I don't think she did, either."

"Tell her, Sam."

"Tell her what?"

A knowing smile curved Paige's lips. "Tell her that you love her, of course."

"OKAY, I GUESS YOU'RE ALL wondering why I've asked you here." Crystal drew a deep breath Saturday morning and smiled at Megs, her mother and her father, who sat stiffly on opposite sides of her kitchen table.

"You said it was important—a matter of life or death." Megs sat, arms crossed, a frown drawing her eyebrows into a deep V.

"Yes, I did. It *is* a matter of life or death. All this bickering and upset of late is killing this family."

Crystal had had another nonstop night of writing. Over the past week, not only had she finished her piece for Sam, she'd also blown through the first two of her makeover articles and she'd outlined the third. She should be exhausted, but excitement strummed along her veins, even in light of the sour expressions gathered before her.

She drew a deep breath and smiled again. It was a real smile, fueled by the confidence swelling inside her. She could do this. She could put first this family, then her own life, to rights.

"I think it says quite a bit that you all showed," she said. "I had my doubts after all the trauma we've experienced over the past week or so, but I knew deep down we'd all find a way to pull back together.''

''Darling, I'm not sure what you hope to accomplish here, but you have to know that it's going to take more than a little family chat to get your mother to talk to me again.'' Her father unfolded his arms and pressed his hands to his knees.

Her mother scowled at him across the table. ''So, this trouble is all my fault?''

''Mom, Dad, and you, too, Megs, please, just listen to me for a minute.'' Crystal waited until all eyes faced her. ''Okay, I've recently finished an article on family reunions and I learned a lot from it that I'd like to share.''

She paused and they all looked to her, expectantly, though with a measure of impatience. She lifted her chin and continued, ''What we have here is a family divided. Mom, you're upset with Dad, and Megs, you're upset with me.''

Her mother and sister grumbled their agreement and shifted in their chairs.

''So, what we need is a little mini family reunion to reunite this family.''

''Honey, do you not remember the last reunion we had with your father's family?'' Her mother gestured to the rest of them and they murmured an acknowledgement. ''What a fiasco. Uncle Don and cousin Barry got into that fist fight and everyone was choosing sides.''

''But there's a better way to have a reunion. That was the wrong way.''

''And the right way would be…?'' Megs looked at her, her eyebrows arched in question.

Crystal beamed at them. ‘‘We blend the old with the new.’’

They stared back at her with blank faces. Her father shook his head. ‘‘Maybe you should elaborate.’’

‘‘Gladly. Now, we can work with this, but I have a proposal. It's going to mean we'll all have to compromise, but I think we all want to make this work or we wouldn't be here.’’

Again, they each murmured their agreement. Her mother asked, ‘‘So, what's this proposal?’’

‘‘Okay, hear me out, then we can discuss any points you want. First, Dad, you were unhappy with your new job and you didn't see the point in talking to your boss about going back.’’

‘‘That's right. I don't see that VP position as a viable option.’’ He turned to his wife. ‘‘I'm sorry, Sarah, but I'm just not cut out for that corporate life.’’

Before her mother could respond, Crystal hurried on, ‘‘So let's look at how we could blend the old with the new for you. Is there some way you could go back to your old job, but maybe add some responsibilities from the new one that might justify a pay increase and would keep you at the facility level?’’

Her mother leaned forward, Megs uncrossed her arms and a half smile played across her father's lips. Hope flickered in Crystal. Was it going to work?

‘‘I'll have to think about it,’’ he said. ‘‘But maybe…yes, it's possible I could handle some of the special projects on a bonus basis.’’

‘‘Really? That might work?’’ Her mother straightened in her chair.

‘‘I don't know. I'll have to talk to Bannon, see what he thinks.’’ He faced Crystal. ‘‘But it's not a bad plan.'' He frowned again. ''I'm not sure that would mean we could still get the house, though.''

''But we'll still try, right?'' Her mother folded her arms.

''It won't be easy.'' Her father rose, then paced, furrows lining his forehead.

Crystal's heart sank. She turned to her mother. ''Maybe you could find a way to compromise?''

''It could work,'' Megs said.

They all turned to her and she continued, ''You keep the old house, but you renovate it—make it into a like-new house.''

Her mother's gaze narrowed. ''I'd want the same carpet and wall coverings I ordered for the new house. And that kitchen would have to be gutted and completely remodeled.''

''Would you be happy with that, Sarah?'' Bob took her hand in his.

Her lips thinned, but some of the hardness left her eyes. ''I don't mean to be uncompromising. I just hate to see you sell yourself short. And it hurts that you would make that kind of decision without talking to me first. I don't think you've given the new position enough time. We deserve that house.''

''I'm not saying we don't deserve it. I'm saying we may no longer qualify for it.''

''I *know* what you're saying and we'd qualify if you'd go back to your new job.''

Crystal's father threw up his hands in frustration. ''Will you at least think about the possibility of staying in the old house and renovating?''

For a long moment, his wife stared at him, her lips pursed. ''I'll think about it.''

Crystal let out her breath. It was a start and perhaps the best she'd get from her mother right now. She turned to her sister. "Okay, Megs, I don't really know how to use this to fix things between us—"

Megs held up her hand. "I accused you of making yourself into something you're not, but I should have been talking to myself. I was just so jealous of you. You have such passion in you and you're free spirited. I think I just wanted to know what it would be like to live like you do, to let my impulses drive me.

"You were right, Crystal, about Leo. I'm really sorry about everything I said. I should never have let that whole wedding fiasco—"

"Wedding fiasco?" their parents asked in unison.

Megs waved to them. "We'll fill each other in later. I didn't know about the whole job-house fiasco, either."

"I have a series of articles I'm writing on makeovers." Crystal twisted her napkin. "They're not your standard makeover articles. I incorporated the blending-of-the-old-with-the-new theme and I like the way it turned out. I think I had trouble with it at first, because I, like you, Mom, was too focused on the more obvious stuff.

"But with all that's happened, I started to look at myself and I found that makeovers are not only skin deep, or they don't have to be. It *is* possible to make over the deeper aspects of your personality. I think I've found a way to blend that impulsive side of me with the new improved me, who takes things a little more seriously."

Megs beamed at her. "So, you're writing articles of depth?"

Pride expanded Crystal's chest as she smiled back at her sister. "I'm giving it my best shot. And I think it's time I added a little depth to the rest of my life as well."

CHASING RAINBOWS. Sam stared at the title of Crystal's article, then reread the paragraphs beneath. It was good. Damn good. He'd forwarded it to his father over an hour ago. The old man was bound to love it.

But suddenly his father's approval seemed unimportant. Whether he granted Sam the controlling interest or not didn't matter. The content of her article suddenly took front stage in his mind. His heart thudded and his palms sweated. She'd realized that getting her pot of gold hadn't met her expectations.

Had she truly gotten over her infatuation with Kincaid?

Sam picked up the phone, dialed, then waited through four rings until her answering machine picked up. He slammed down the receiver. Had she gone away with Kincaid, after all, or was she home writing and too busy to answer her phone?

He had to know. Drawing a deep breath, he headed for his bedroom. He'd stop by her apartment, then if she wasn't home he'd head for the beach. And wherever, whenever, he found her he'd lay it all on the line. It was time he let her know exactly how he felt. First, he needed to get dressed.

Moments later, he ran a comb through his hair, then shook his head and scrubbed his fingers over his scalp, disrupting the neat furrows. Damn his hair. It would have to do.

He left the bathroom and strode into his bedroom.

Nearly every piece of clothing he owned lay strewn about on the bed, the chair or the dresser. Swearing softly, he picked up a pair of slacks and a dress shirt. What did one wear to proclaim one's love?

Damn it, damn it, his heart raced like a boxcar and he sweated like a horse. He tossed down the dress clothes and grabbed up a T-shirt and jeans. They would have to do, even though Crystal would probably be dressed to kill for her weekend with Kincaid.

He closed his eyes and prayed he wasn't too late. Crashing Kincaid's beach house was an act of desperation, but Sam was a desperate man. And he meant to tell Crystal all he felt for her, if it killed and even humiliated him.

He'd just have to get used to her new calendar-model image. *If* she'd have anything to do with him, that is, if he actually ruined her weekend to lay his heart on the line.

His front bell rang as he slipped into his jeans. Carrying the T-shirt, he padded barefoot to answer the summons, cursing whatever solicitor might be calling at this hour. Glaring, he yanked open the door.

"Hello, Sam." Crystal stood on his front step.

He blinked and his heart quickened. This was no calendar model. This was the Crystal of old, with her ripped jeans and faded T-shirt. A ball cap sat backward on her head.

But there was something new about this old Crystal. She radiated the sex appeal and sensuality of her new calendar alter ego. The combination nearly brought him to his knees.

"Crystal..." He stood in the open door, drinking in the sight of her.

"Aren't you going to ask me in?"

"Jes— Yes, come in. Please, come in." He stepped aside and she breezed by him, her scent tantalizing and clean.

She hooked her thumbs in her belt loops and turned to him, her gaze sweeping him from head to toe, then back again. "So, do you still want to hit the ball field?"

The ball field? How could she think about sports when he was about to burst into flames? "I—I was just going to come see you. I read the article. It's perfect. Why aren't you with Kincaid?"

A smile of pure joy lit her face. "You were? You were heading for Ron's beach house, because you thought I was there?"

"I was going to stop by your place first, in case you were there."

"Why?" she asked.

"Why?"

"Yes. Why were you coming to see me? And why did you think I might be with Ron?" She moved in close to him, ran her hand along his bare chest, sending shivers of arousal to his every nerve ending.

He stared blankly at the shirt he clutched in his hand. With a shake of his head, he tossed it aside. "He said he was going to offer you a spot in the calendar—ask you to spend the weekend with him."

"I turned down the calendar...and the weekend with Ron."

"You did?" A wide grin curved his lips. She *hadn't* wanted to be with Kincaid.

"So..." She brushed her cheek along his. "Why were you coming to see me?"

His pulse thudded in his ears. ''I—I have something very important to tell you.''

''You do?'' She drew back. Her impossibly blue eyes widened. She gazed at him expectantly.

A bead of sweat trickled down his temple. He closed his eyes and drew a deep breath. Then he fastened his gaze on hers. ''I love you, Crystal. I always have. God help me, I always will.''

Tears welled in her eyes and for a split second he stood horrified. He'd hurt her—done or said something wrong. But then she laughed and threw her arms around his neck. She rained kisses over his cheeks, his nose.

Profound relief washed over him and he held her close and whispered those magic words again. ''I love you.''

''Oh, Sam, I love you, too.''

Joy burst over him and he kissed her again, taking his time to enjoy all her sweetness he'd missed over the past weeks. He pulled back and grinned at her. ''You do, really? You love me?''

''With all my heart.''

He sobered. ''Crystal, I've been thinking. That article was great—edgy, interesting, everything I knew it would be, but you don't have to do the column. I don't care about the controlling interest—''

''What controlling interest?''

''Oh.'' He frowned. ''My father promised me the controlling interest in the magazine, if I could get you to write the column and make it fly.''

''Really?'' Her eyes narrowed.

He hurried on. ''Yeah, but none of that matters. I just want you to write what you're comfortable writing. I can live with the magazine as it is, at least for a while. I can always find another writer. I trust my father's judgment. If he's so opposed to change, then maybe he's got his reasons."

"I've already got some ideas for more articles. I've got a notepad full of notes."

"You do?"

She nodded. "I think it's time."

"Time for what?"

"Time to add a little depth to my life."

"You mean the column?"

"Yes, and I mean my relationships, too."

"Ah, a relationship of depth."

"Yeah, you interested?"

"Hell, yes."

She slid her mouth over his, teasing him with the softness of her lips. "So, are you ready?"

"For what?"

"For this."

She moved away from him and whipped the ball cap off her head. Her platinum waves spilled down around her shoulders. She slipped off her shoes, then slowly undid her jeans. His breath caught as she stepped from the denim to reveal soft cotton boxers.

"Oh, babe..." He hoisted her into his arms. "You just don't know what you do to me."

"I think I have some idea." She laughed lightly and nuzzled his neck.

He strode into the bedroom, then deposited her on the bed, on top of a pile of clothes. She laughed again and scooped an armload onto the floor. "What is all this?"

"I couldn't decide what to wear."

Her heated gaze swept over his bare chest and jeans. "You chose wisely. Except..."

She shook her head as she unbuttoned his jeans. His fly rasped in the quiet room. Then she slipped the garment down his legs, over his feet, to reveal his own plaid boxers.

She sighed, "Much better."

With a playful growl, he lunged on top of her. Her laughter sent warmth curling through him as he stripped off her shirt, then placed kisses all over her chest and sports bra. He pulled her close and kissed her long and deep, her mouth hot and hungry beneath his, the softness of her body molding to him, like a missing half.

"Too many clothes," he said, when they finally broke for air.

Her gaze burned into his as she slipped off the rest of her clothes. He quickly followed suit, stripping off his boxers, then stretching out beside her to run his hand up, then down her length. The blue of her eyes held him transfixed.

"Love me, Crystal."

As gentle as a soft rain, she drew him toward her. Her kiss was the sweetest he'd ever tasted, her touch ignited a fire in him that only she could douse. He kissed her breast, laving her nipple into a hard bead, then parted her thighs and dipped his fingers into the well of her desire.

She shifted to reach into his nightstand, then she held a square packet before him. He smiled, took it from her and readied himself. "We need to plan something else, so we don't have to always disrupt the flow. I want to know the feel of your body and mine, with nothing between us."

"Yes, that'll be heaven." Her words ended in a moan as he slipped inside her.

She met him stroke for stroke as he set the pace to love her through the afternoon, then well into the night. They had all the time they needed now. Time to love.

Her muscles tightened around him and he moved over her, inside her, her heat gloving him, sending ripples of pleasure throughout him. He grasped both her hands and held her gaze as he thrust deep inside her.

They needed no words to follow the flow of their lovemaking as desire gripped them. He moved and she responded, her eyes widening as the tremors of her orgasm claimed her.

He cried her name, caught in the sweetest release.

Sometime, much later, in the wee morning hours as they lay sated, entangled in each other's arms, she turned to him.

"Sam?"

"Yes?" He rolled to his side and smiled at her. She was his, truly his.

"Remember when you said that when I'd gotten all I wanted out of this whole makeover business, then I could thank you?"

He nodded and traced his finger along the curve of her cheek, a cheek he meant to spend a lifetime admiring.

She smiled that sexy smile of hers that had his toes curling and his heart swelling and said, "Well…thank you."

In April, bestselling author

Tori Carrington

introduces a provocative miniseries
that gives new meaning to the word *scandal!*

Sleeping with Secrets

Don't miss

FORBIDDEN April 2004

INDECENT June 2004

WICKED August 2004

Sleeping with Secrets

Sex has never been so shamelessly gratifying....

Available wherever Harlequin books are sold.

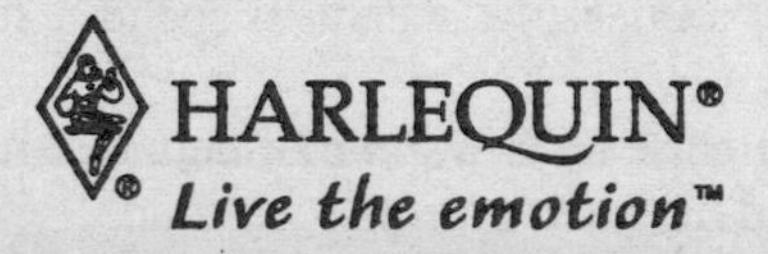

www.eHarlequin.com

HBSWS